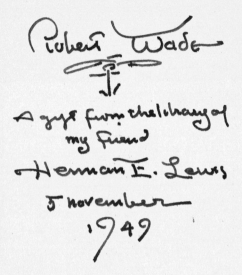

Robert Wade
Jr.

A gift from the library of
my friend

Herman E. Lewis

5 november
1949

FALK
AMY FOSTER
TO-MORROW
THREE STORIES
BY
JOSEPH CONRAD

NEW YORK
McCLURE, PHILLIPS
AND COMPANY
MCMIII

CONTENTS

FALK

A REMINISCENCE

FALK

A REMINISCENCE

Several of us, all more or less connected with the
sea, were dining in a small river-hostelry not more
than thirty miles from London, and less than twenty
from that shallow and dangerous puddle to which
our coasting men give the grandiose name of " German Ocean." And through the wide windows we
had a view of the Thames; an enfilading view down
the Lower Hope Reach. But the dinner was exe-
crable, and all the feast was for the eyes.

That flavour of salt-water which for so many of
us had been the very water of life permeated our
talk. He who hath known the bitterness of the
Ocean shall have its taste forever in his mouth. But
one or two of us, pampered by the life of the land,
complained of hunger. It was impossible to swal-
low any of that stuff. And indeed there was a
strange mustiness in everything. The wooden dining-room stuck out over the mud of the shore like

[3]

a lacustrine dwelling; the planks of the floor seemed rotten; a decrepid old waiter tottered pathetically to and fro before an antediluvian and worm-eaten sideboard; the chipped plates might have been disinterred from some kitchen midden near an inhabited lake; and the chops recalled times more ancient still. They brought forcibly to one's mind the night of ages when the primeval man, evolving the first rudiments of cookery from his dim consciousness, scorched lumps of flesh at a fire of sticks in the company of other good fellows; then, gorged and happy, sat him back among the gnawed bones to tell his artless tales of experience—the tales of hunger and hunt—and of women, perhaps!

But luckily the wine happened to be as old as the waiter. So, comparatively empty, but upon the whole fairly happy, we sat back and told our artless tales. We talked of the sea and all its works. The sea never changes, and its works for all the talk of men are wrapped in mystery. But we agreed that the times were changed. And we talked of old ships, of sea-accidents, of break-downs, dismastings; and of a man who brought his ship safe to Liverpool all the way from the River Platte under a jury rudder. We talked of wrecks, of short rations and of heroism—or at least of what the newspapers would have called heroism at sea—a manifestation of virtues quite different from the heroism of primitive times. And now and then falling silent all together we gazed at the sights of the river.

A P. & O. boat passed bound down. " One gets jolly good dinners on board these ships," remarked one of our band. A man with sharp eyes read out the name on her bows: *Arcadia*. "What a beautiful model of a ship!" murmured some of us. She was followed by a small cargo steamer, and the flag they hauled down aboard while we were looking showed her to be a Norwegian. She made an awful lot of smoke; and before it had quite blown away, a high-sided, short, wooden barque, in ballast and towed by a paddle-tug, appeared in front of the windows. All her hands were forward busy setting up the headgear; and aft a woman in a red hood, quite alone with the man at the wheel, paced the length of the poop back and forth, with the grey wool of some knitting work in her hands.

" German I should think," muttered one. " The skipper has his wife on board," remarked another;

[5]

and the light of the crimson sunset all ablaze behind the London smoke, throwing a glow of Bengal light upon the barque's spars, faded away from the Hope Reach.

Then one of us, who had not spoken before, a man of over fifty, that had commanded ships for a quarter of a century, looking after the barque now gliding far away, all black on the lustre of the river, said:

This reminds me of an absurd episode in my life, now many years ago, when I got first the command of an iron barque, loading then in a certain Eastern seaport. It was also the capital of an Eastern kingdom, lying up a river as might be London lies up this old Thames of ours. No more need be said of the place; for this sort of thing might have happened anywhere where there are ships, skippers, tugboats, and orphan nieces of indescribable splendour. And the absurdity of the episode concerns only me, my enemy Falk, and my friend Hermann.

There seemed to be something like peculiar emphasis on the words " My friend Hermann," which caused one of us (for we had just been speaking of heroism at sea) to say idly and nonchalantly:

[6]

FALK

" And was this Hermann a hero? "

Not at all, said our grizzled friend. No hero at all. He was a Schiff-führer: Ship-conductor. That's how they call a Master Mariner in Germany. I prefer our way. The alliteration is good, and there is something in the nomenclature that gives to us as a body the sense of corporate existence: Apprentice, Mate, Master, in the ancient and honourable craft of the sea. As to my friend Hermann, he might have been a consummate master of the honourable craft, but he was called officially Schiff-führer, and had the simple, heavy appearance of a well-to-do farmer, combined with the good-natured shrewdness of a small shopkeeper. With his shaven chin, round limbs, and heavy eyelids he did not look like a toiler, and even less like an adventurer of the sea. Still, he toiled upon the seas, in his own way, much as a shopkeeper works behind his counter. And his ship was the means by which he maintained his growing family.

She was a heavy, strong, blunt-bowed affair, awakening the ideas of primitive solidity, like the wooden plough of our forefathers. And there were, about her, other suggestions of a rustic and homely

[7]

nature. The extraordinary timber projections which I have seen in no other vessel made her square stern resemble the tail end of a miller's waggon. But the four stern ports of her cabin, glazed with six little greenish panes each, and framed in wooden sashes painted brown, might have been the windows of a cottage in the country. The tiny white curtains and the greenery of flower pots behind the glass completed the resemblance. On one or two occasions when passing under her stern I had detected from my boat a round arm in the act of tilting a watering pot, and the bowed sleek head of a maiden whom I shall always call Hermann's niece, because as a matter of fact I've never heard her name, for all my intimacy with the family.

This, however, sprang up later on. Meantime in common with the rest of the shipping in that Eastern port, I was left in no doubt as to Hermann's notions of hygienic clothing. Evidently he believed in wearing good stout flannel next his skin. On most days little frocks and pinafores could be seen drying in the mizzen rigging of his ship, or a tiny row of socks fluttering on the signal halyards; but once a fortnight the family washing was exhibited

[8]

in force. It covered the poop entirely. The afternoon breeze would incite to a weird and flabby activ-
ity all that crowded mass of clothing, with its vague
suggestions of drowned, mutilated and flattened humanity. Trunks without heads waved at you arms
without hands; legs without feet kicked fantasti-
cally with collapsible flourishes; and there were long
white garments that, taking the wind fairly
through their neck openings edged with lace, became for a moment violently distended as by the
passage of obese and invisible bodies. On these days
you could make out that ship at a great distance
by the multi-coloured grotesque riot going on abaft
her mizzen mast.

She had her berth just ahead of me, and her
name was *Diana*,—Diana not of Ephesus but of
Bremen. This was proclaimed in white letters a
foot long spaced widely across the stern (somewhat
like the lettering of a shop-sign) under the cottage
windows. This ridiculously unsuitable name struck
one as an impertinence towards the memory of the
most charming of goddesses; for, apart from the
fact that the old craft was physically incapable of
engaging in any sort of chase, there was a gang of

four children belonging to her. They peeped over the rail at passing boats and occasionally dropped various objects into them. Thus, sometime before I knew Hermann to speak to, I received on my hat a horrid rag-doll belonging to Hermann's eldest daughter. However, these youngsters were upon the whole well behaved. They had fair heads, round eyes, round little knobby noses, and they resembled their father a good deal.

This *Diana* of Bremen was a most innocent old ship, and seemed to know nothing of the wicked sea, as there are on shore households that know nothing of the corrupt world. And the sentiments she suggested were unexceptionable and mainly of a domestic order. She was a home. All these dear children had learned to walk on her roomy quarter-deck. In such thoughts there is something pretty, even touching. Their teeth, I should judge, they had cut on the ends of her running gear. I have many times observed the baby Hermann (Nicholas) engaged in gnawing the whipping of the fore-royal brace. Nicholas' favourite place of residence was under the main fife-rail. Directly he was let loose he would crawl off there, and the first seaman who came along would bring him, carefully held aloft in tarry hands, back to the cabin door. I fancy there must have been a standing order to that effect. In the course of these transportations the baby, who was the only peppery person in the ship, tried to smite these stalwart young German sailors on the face.

Mrs. Hermann, an engaging, stout housewife, wore on board baggy blue dresses with white dots. When, as happened once or twice I caught her at an elegant little wash-tub rubbing hard on white collars, baby's socks, and Hermann's summer neckties, she would blush in girlish confusion, and raising her wet hands greet me from afar with many friendly nods. Her sleeves would be rolled up to the elbows, and the gold hoop of her wedding ring glittered among the soapsuds. Her voice was pleasant, she had a serene brow, smooth bands of very fair hair, and a good-humoured expression of the eyes. She was motherly and moderately talkative. When this simple matron smiled, youthful dimples broke out on her fresh broad cheeks. Hermann's niece on the other hand, an orphan and very silent, I never saw attempt a smile. This, however,

[11]

was not gloom on her part but the restraint of youthful gravity.

They had carried her about with them for the last three years, to help with the children and be company for Mrs. Hermann, as Hermann mentioned once to me. It had been very necessary while they were all little, he had added in a vexed manner. It was her arm and her sleek head that I had glimpsed one morning, through the stern-windows of the cabin, hovering over the pots of fuchsias and mignonette; but the first time I beheld her full length I surrendered to her proportions. They fix her in my mind, as great beauty, great intelligence, quickness of wit or kindness of heart might have made some other woman equally memorable.

With her it was form and size. It was her physical personality that had this imposing charm. She might have been witty, intelligent, and kind to an exceptional degree. I don't know, and this is not to the point. All I know is that she was built on a magnificent scale. Built is the only word. She was constructed, she was erected, as it were, with a regal lavishness. It staggered you to see this reckless expenditure of material upon a chit of a girl. She was youthful and also perfectly mature, as though she had been some fortunate immortal. She was heavy too, perhaps, but that's nothing. It only added to that notion of permanence. She was barely nineteen. But such shoulders! Such round arms! Such a shadowing forth of mighty limbs when with three long strides she pounced across the deck upon the overturned Nicholas—it's perfectly indescribable! She seemed a good, quiet girl, vigilant as to Lena's needs, Gustav's tumbles, the state of Carl's dear little nose—conscientious, hardworking, and all that. But what magnificent hair she had! Abundant, long, thick, of a tawny colour. It had the sheen of precious metals. She wore it plaited tightly into one single tress hanging girlishly down her back and its end reached down to her waist. The massiveness of it surprised you. On my word it reminded one of a club. Her face was big, comely, of an unruffled expression. She had a good complexion, and her blue eyes were so pale that she appeared to look at the world with the empty white candour of a statue. You could not call her good-looking. It was something much more impressive. The simplicity of her apparel,

[13]

the opulence of her form, her imposing stature, and the extraordinary sense of vigorous life that seemed to emanate from her like a perfume exhaled by a flower, made her beautiful with a beauty of a rustic and olympian order. To watch her reaching up to the clothes-line with both arms raised high above her head, caused you to fall a musing in a strain of pagan piety. Excellent Mrs. Hermann's baggy cotton gowns had some sort of rudimentary frills at neck and bottom, but this girl's print frocks hadn't even a wrinkle; nothing but a few straight folds in the skirt falling to her feet, and these, when she stood still, had a severe and statuesque quality. She was inclined naturally to be still whether sitting or standing. However, I don't mean to say she was statuesque. She was too generously alive: but she could have stood for an allegoric statue of the Earth. I don't mean the worn-out earth of our possession, but a young Earth, a virginal planet undisturbed by the vision of a future teeming with the monstrous forms of life and death, clamorous with the cruel battles of hunger and thought.

The worthy Hermann himself was not very entertaining, though his English was fairly compre-

FALK

hensible. Mrs. Hermann, who always let off one
speech at least at me in an hospitable, cordial tone
(and in Platt-Deutsch I suppose) I could not understand. As to their niece, however satisfactory
to look upon (and she inspired you somehow with
a hopeful view as to the prospects of mankind)
she was a modest and silent presence, mostly engaged in sewing, only now and then, as I observed,
falling over that work into a state of maidenly
meditation. Her aunt sat opposite her, sewing also,
with her feet propped on a wooden footstool. On
the other side of the deck Hermann and I would
get a couple of chairs out of the cabin and settle
down to a smoking match, accompanied at long in-
tervals by the pacific exchange of a few words. I
came nearly every evening. Hermann I would find
in his shirt sleeves. As soon as he returned from
the shore on board his ship he commenced operations
by taking off his coat; then he put on his head an
embroidered round cap with a tassel, and changed
his boots for a pair of cloth slippers. Afterwards
he smoked at the cabin-door, looking at his children
with an air of civic virtue, till they got caught one
after another and put to bed in various staterooms.

[15]

Lastly, we would drink some beer in the cabin, which was furnished with a wooden table on cross legs, and with black straight-backed chairs—more like a farm kitchen than a ship's cuddy. The sea and all nautical affairs seemed very far removed from the hospitality of this exemplary family.

And I liked this because I had a rather worrying time on board my own ship. I had been appointed ex-officio by the British Consul to take charge of her after a man who had died suddenly, leaving for the guidance of his successor some suspiciously unreceipted bills, a few dry-dock estimates hinting at bribery, and a quantity of vouchers for three years' extravagant expenditure; all these mixed up together in a dusty old violin-case lined with ruby velvet. I found besides a large account-book, which, when opened, hopefully turned out to my infinite consternation to be filled with verses—page after page of rhymed doggerel of a jovial and improper character, written in the neatest minute hand I ever did see. In the same fiddle-case a photograph of my predecessor, taken lately in Saigon, represented in front of a garden view, and in company of a female in strange draperies, an elderly, squat, rugged man of stern aspect in a clumsy suit of black broadcloth, and with the hair brushed forward above the temples in a manner reminding one of a boar's tusks. Of a fiddle, however, the only trace on board was the case, its empty husk as it were; but of the two last freights the ship had indubitably earned of late, there were not even the husks left. It was impossible to say where all that money had gone to. It wasn't on board. It had not been remitted home; for a letter from the owners, preserved in a desk evidently by the merest accident, complained mildly enough that they had not been favoured by a scratch of the pen for the last eighteen months. There were next to no stores on board, not an inch of spare rope or a yard of canvas. The ship had been run bare, and I foresaw no end of difficulties before I could get her ready for sea.

As I was young then—not thirty yet—I took myself and my troubles very seriously. The old mate, who had acted as chief mourner at the captain's funeral, was not particularly pleased at my coming. But the fact is the fellow was not legally qualified for command, and the Consul was bound, if at all possible, to put a properly certificated man on board. As to the second mate, all I can say his name was Tottersen, or something like that. His practice was to wear on his head, in that tropical climate, a mangy fur cap. He was, without exception, the stupidest man I had ever seen on board ship. And he looked it too. He looked so confoundedly stupid that it was a matter of surprise for me when he answered to his name.

I drew no great comfort from their company, to say the least of it; while the prospect of making a long sea passage with those two fellows was depressing. And my other thoughts in solitude could not be of a gay complexion. The crew was sickly, the cargo was coming very slow; I foresaw I would have lots of trouble with the charterers, and doubted whether they would advance me enough money for the ship's expenses. Their attitude towards me was unfriendly. Altogether I was not getting on. I would discover at odd times (generally about midnight) that I was totally inexperienced, greatly ignorant of business, and hopelessly unfit for any sort of command; and when the steward had to be taken to the hospital ill with choleraic symptoms I felt bereaved of the only decent person at the after end of the ship. He was fully expected to recover, but in the meantime had to be replaced by some sort of servant. And on the recommendation of a certain Schomberg, the proprietor of the smaller of the two hotels in the place, I engaged a Chinaman. Schomberg, a brawny, hairy Alsatian, and an awful gossip, assured me that it was all right. " First-class boy that. Came in the *suite* of his Excellency Tseng the Commissioner—you know. His Excellency Tseng lodged with me here for three weeks."

He mouthed the Chinese Excellency at me with great unction, though the specimen of the " *suite* " did not seem very promising. At the time, however, I did not know what an untrustworthy humbug Schomberg was. The " boy " might have been forty or a hundred and forty for all you could tell— one of those Chinamen of the death's-head type of face and completely inscrutable. Before the end of the third day he had revealed himself as a confirmed opium-smoker, a gambler, a most audacious thief, and a first-class sprinter. When he departed at the top of his speed with thirty-two golden sovereigns of my own hard-earned savings it was the last straw. I had reserved that money in case my difficulties

came to the worst. Now it was gone I felt as poor
and naked as a fakir. I clung to my ship, for all
the bother she caused me, but what I could not bear
were the long lonely evenings in her cuddy, where
the atmosphere, made smelly by a leaky lamp, was
agitated by the snoring of the mate. That fellow
shut himself up in his stuffy cabin punctually at
eight, and made gross and revolting noises like a
water-logged trump. It was odious not to be able
to worry oneself in comfort on board one's own
ship. Everything in this world, I reflected, even
the command of a nice little barque, may be made
a delusion and a snare for the unwary spirit of
pride in man.

From such reflections I was glad to make any escape on board that Bremen *Diana*. There apparently no whisper of the world's iniquities had ever
penetrated. And yet she lived upon the wide sea:
and the sea tragic and comic, the sea with its horrors
and its peculiar scandals, the sea peopled by men
and ruled by iron necessity is indubitably a part of
the world. But that patriarchal old tub, like some
saintly retreat, echoed nothing of it. She was world
proof. Her venerable innocence apparently had

put a restraint on the roaring lusts of the sea. And yet I have known the sea too long to believe in its respect for decency. An elemental force is ruthlessly frank. It may, of course, have been Hermann's skilful seamanship, but to me it looked as if the allied oceans had refrained from smashing these high bulwarks, unshipping the lumpy rudder, frightening the children, and generally opening this family's eyes out of sheer reticence. It looked like reticence. The ruthless disclosure was in the end left for a man to make; a man strong and elemental enough and driven to unveil some secrets of the sea by the power of a simple and elemental desire.

This, however, occurred much later, and meantime I took sanctuary in that serene old ship early every evening. The only person on board that seemed to be in trouble was little Lena, and in due course I perceived that the health of the rag-doll was more than delicate. This object led a sort of " in extremis " existence in a wooden box placed against the starboard mooring-bitts, tended and nursed with the greatest sympathy and care by all the children, who greatly enjoyed pulling long faces and moving with hushed footsteps. Only the baby

—Nicholas—looked on with a cold, ruffianly leer, as if he had belonged to another tribe altogether. Lena perpetually sorrowed over the box, and all of them were in deadly earnest. It was wonderful the way these children would work up their compassion for that bedraggled thing I wouldn't have touched with a pair of tongs. I suppose they were exercising and developing their racial sentimentalism by the means of that dummy. I was only surprised that Mrs. Hermann let Lena cherish and hug that bundle of rags to that extent, it was so disreputably and completely unclean. But Mrs. Hermann would raise her fine womanly eyes from her needlework to look on with amused sympathy, and did not seem to see it, somehow, that this object of affection was a disgrace to the ship's purity. Purity, not cleanliness, is the word. It was pushed so far that I seemed to detect in this too a sentimental excess, as if dirt had been removed in very love. It is impossible to give you an idea of such a meticulous neatness. It was as if every morning that ship had been arduously explored with—with toothbrushes. Her very bowsprit three times a week had its toilette made with a cake of soap and a piece of soft flannel. Arrayed—I *must* say arrayed—arrayed artlessly in dazzling white paint as to wood and dark green as to ironwork the simple-minded distribution of these colours evoked the images of simple-minded peace, of arcadian felicity; and the childish comedy of disease and sorrow struck me sometimes as an abominably real blot upon that ideal state.

I enjoyed it greatly, and on my part I brought a little mild excitement into it. Our intimacy arose from the pursuit of that thief. It was in the evening, and Hermann, who, contrary to his habits, had stayed on shore late that day, was extricating himself backwards out of a little gharry on the river bank, opposite his ship, when the hunt passed. Realising the situation as though he had eyes in his shoulder-blades, he joined us with a leap and took the lead. The Chinaman fled silent like a rapid shadow on the dust of an extremely oriental road. I followed. A long way in the rear my mate whooped like a savage. A young moon threw a bashful light on a plain like a monstrous waste ground: the architectural mass of a Buddhist temple far away projected itself in dead black on the sky. We lost the thief of course; but in my disap-

[23]

pointment I had to admire Hermann's presence of mind. The velocity that stodgy man developed in the interests of a complete stranger earned my warm gratitude—there was something truly cordial in his exertions.

He seemed as vexed as myself at our failure, and would hardly listen to my thanks. He said it was " nothings," and invited me on the spot to come on board his ship and drink a glass of beer with him. We poked sceptically for a while amongst the bushes, peered without conviction into a ditch or two. There was not a sound : patches of slime glim-mered feebly amongst the reeds. Slowly we trudged back, drooping under the thin sickle of the moon, and I heard him mutter to himself, " Himmel! Zwei und dreissig Pfund! " He was impressed by the figure of my loss. For a long time we had ceased to hear the mate's whoops and yells.

Then he said to me, " Everybody has his troub-les," and as we went on remarked that he would never have known anything of mine hadn't he by an extraordinary chance been detained on shore by Captain Falk. He didn't like to stay late ashore— he added with a sigh. The something doleful in his tone I put to his sympathy with my misfortune, of course.

On board the *Diana* Mrs. Hermann's fine eyes expressed much interest and commiseration. We had found the two women sewing face to face under the open skylight in the strong glare of the lamp. Hermann walked in first, starting in the very doorway to pull off his coat, and encouraging me with loud, hospitable ejaculations: "Come in! This way! Come in, captain!" At once, coat in hand, he began to tell his wife all about it. Mrs. Hermann put the palms of her plump hands together; I smiled and bowed with a heavy heart: the niece got up from her sewing to bring Hermann's slippers and his embroidered calotte, which he assumed pontifically, talking (about me) all the time. Billows of white stuff lay between the chairs on the cabin floor; I caught the words "Zwei und dreissig Pfund" repeated several times, and presently came the beer, which seemed delicious to my throat, parched with running and the emotions of the chase.

I didn't get away till well past midnight, long after the women had retired. Hermann had been trading in the East for three years or more, carry-

ing freights of rice and timber mostly. His ship
was well known in all the ports from Vladivostok to
Singapore. She was his own property. The profits
had been moderate, but the trade answered well
enough while the children were small yet. In another year or so he hoped he would be able to sell the
old *Diana* to a firm in Japan for a fair price. He
intended to return home, to Bremen, by mail boat,
second class, with Mrs. Hermann and the children.
He told me all this stolidly, with slow puffs at his
pipe. I was sorry when knocking the ashes out he
began to rub his eyes. I would have sat with him
till morning. What had I to hurry on board my
own ship for? To face the broken rifled drawer in
my state-room. Ugh! The very thought made me
feel unwell.

I became their daily guest, as you know. I think
that Mrs. Hermann from the first looked upon me
as a romantic person. I did not, of course, tear my
hair *coram populo* over my loss, and she took it for
lordly indifference. Afterwards, I daresay, I did
tell them some of my adventures—such as they were
—and they marvelled greatly at the extent of my
experience. Hermann would translate what he

thought the most striking passages. Getting up on his legs, and as if delivering a lecture on a phenomenon, he addressed himself, with gestures, to the two women, who would let their sewing sink slowly on their laps. Meantime I sat before a glass of Hermann's beer, trying to look modest. Mrs. Hermann would glance at me quickly, emit slight " Ach's ! " The girl never made a sound. Never. But she too would sometimes raise her pale eyes to look at me in her unseeing gentle way. Her glance was by no means stupid ; it beamed out soft and diffuse as the moon beams upon a landscape—quite differently from the scrutinising inspection of the stars. You were drowned in it, and imagined yourself to appear blurred. And yet this same glance when turned upon Christian Falk must have been as efficient as the searchlight of a battle-ship.

Falk was the other assiduous visitor on board, but from his behaviour he might have been coming to see the quarter-deck capstan. He certainly used to stare at it a good deal when keeping us company outside the cabin door, with one muscular arm thrown over the back of the chair, and his big shapely legs, in very tight white trousers, extended far out and ending in a pair of black shoes as roomy as punts. On arrival he would shake Hermann's hand with a mutter, bow to the women, and take up his careless and misanthropic attitude by our side. He departed abruptly, with a jump, going through the performance of grunts, hand-shakes, bow, as if in a panic. Sometimes, with a sort of discreet and convulsive effort, he approached the women and exchanged a few low words with them, half a dozen at most. On these occasions Hermann's usual stare became positively glassy and Mrs. Hermann's kind countenance would colour up. The girl herself never turned a hair.

Falk was a Dane or perhaps a Norwegian, I can't tell now. At all events he was a Scandinavian of some sort, and a bloated monopolist to boot. It is possible he was unacquainted with the word, but he had a clear perception of the thing itself. His tariff of charges for towing ships in and out was the most brutally inconsiderate document of the sort I had ever seen. He was the commander and owner of the only tug-boat on the river, a very trim white craft of 150 tons or more, as elegantly neat as a yacht, with a round wheel-house rising like a glazed turret high above her sharp bows, and with one slender varnished pole mast forward. I daresay there are yet a few shipmasters afloat who remember Falk and his tug very well. He extracted his pound and a half of flesh from each of us merchant-skippers with an inflexible sort of indifference which made him detested and even feared. Schomberg used to remark: " I won't talk about the fellow. I don't think he has six drinks from year's end to year's end in my place. But my advice is, gentlemen, don't you have anything to do with him, if you can help it."

This advice, apart from unavoidable business relations, was easy to follow because Falk intruded upon no one. It seems absurd to compare a tugboat skipper to a centaur: but he reminded me somehow of an engraving in a little book I had as a boy, which represented centaurs at a stream, and there was one, especially in the foreground, prancing bow and arrows in hand, with regular severe features and an immense curled wavy beard, flowing down his breast. Falk's face reminded me of that centaur. Besides, he was a composite creature. Not a man-horse, it is true, but a man-boat. He lived on board his tug, which was always dashing up and down the river from early morn till dewy eve.

In the last rays of the setting sun, you could pick out far away down the reach his beard borne high up on the white structure, foaming up stream to anchor for the night. There was the white-clad man's body, and the rich brown patch of the hair, and nothing below the waist but the 'thwart-ship white lines of the bridge-screens, that lead the eye to the sharp white lines of the bows cleaving the muddy water of the river.

Separated from his boat to me at least he seemed incomplete. The tug herself without his head and torso on the bridge looked mutilated as it were. But he left her very seldom. All the time I remained in harbour I saw him only twice on shore. On the first occasion it was at my charterers, where he came in misanthropically to get paid for towing out a French barque the day before. The second time I could hardly believe my eyes, for I beheld him reclining under his beard in a cane-bottomed chair in the billiard-room of Schomberg's hotel.

It was very funny to see Schomberg ignoring him pointedly. The artificiality of it contrasted strongly with Falk's natural unconcern. The big Alsatian talked loudly with his other customers, going from one little table to the other, and passing Falk's place of repose with his eyes fixed straight ahead. Falk sat there with an untouched glass at his elbow. He must have known by sight and name every white man in the room, but he never addressed a word to anybody. He acknowledged my presence by a drop of his eyelids, and that was all. Sprawling there in the chair, he would, now and again, draw the palms of both his hands down his face, giving at the same time a slight, almost imperceptible, shudder.

It was a habit he had, and of course I was perfectly familiar with it, since you could not remain an hour in his company without being made to wonder at such a movement breaking some long period of stillness. It was a passionate and inexplicable gesture. He used to make it at all sorts of times; as likely as not after he had been listening to little Lena's chatter about the suffering doll, for instance. The Hermann children always besieged him about his legs closely, though, in a gentle way, he shrank from them a little. He seemed, however, to feel a great affection for the whole family. For Hermann himself especially. He sought his company. In this case, for instance, he must have been waiting for him, because as soon as he appeared Falk rose hastily, and they went out together. Then Schomberg expounded in my hearing to three or four people his theory that Falk was after Captain Hermann's niece, and asserted confidently that nothing would come of it. It was the same last year when Captain Hermann was loading here, he said.

Naturally, I did not believe Schomberg, but I own that for a time I observed closely what went on. All I discovered was some impatience on Hermann's part. At the sight of Falk, stepping over the gangway, the excellent man would begin to mumble and chew between his teeth something that sounded like German swear-words. However, as I've said, I'm not familiar with the language, and Hermann's soft, round-eyed countenance remained unchanged. Staring stolidly ahead he greeted him with, " Wie gehts," or in English, " How are you? " with a throaty enunciation. The girl would look up for an instant and move her lips slightly: Mrs. Hermann let her hands rest on her lap to talk volubly to him for a minute or so in her pleasant voice before she went on with her sewing again. Falk would throw himself into a chair, stretch his big legs, as like as not draw his hands down his face passionately. As to myself, he was not pointedly impertinent: it was rather as though he could not be bothered with such trifles as my existence; and the truth is that being a monopolist he was under no necessity to be amiable. He was sure to get his own extortionate terms out of me for towage whether he frowned or smiled. As a matter of fact, he did neither: but before many days elapsed he managed to astonish me not a little and to set Schomberg's tongue clacking more than ever.

It came about in this way. There was a shallow bar at the mouth of the river which ought to have been kept down, but the authorities of the State were piously busy gilding afresh the great Buddhist Pagoda just then, and I suppose had no money to spare for dredging operations. I don't know how it may be now, but at the time I speak of that sand-bank was a great nuisance to the shipping. One of its consequences was that vessels of a certain draught of water, like Hermann's or mine, could not

complete their loading in the river. After taking
in as much as possible of their cargo, they had to
go outside to fill up. The whole procedure was an
unmitigated bore. When you thought you had as
much on board as your ship could carry safely over
the bar, you went and gave notice to your agents.
They, in their turn, notified Falk that so-and-so
was ready to go out. Then Falk (ostensibly when it
fitted in with his other work, but, if the truth were
known, simply when his arbitrary spirit moved
him), after ascertaining carefully in the office that
there was enough money to meet his bill, would
come along unsympathetically, glaring at you with
his yellow eyes from the bridge, and would drag you
out dishevelled as to rigging, lumbered as to the
decks, with unfeeling haste, as if to execution. And
he would force you too to take the end of his own
wire hawser, for the use of which there was of course
an extra charge. To your shouted remonstrances
against that extortion this towering trunk with one
hand on the engine-room telegraph only shook its
bearded head above the splash, the racket, and the
clouds of smoke in which the tug, backing and filling in the smother of churning paddle-wheels be-

haved like a ferocious and impatient creature. He
had her manned by the cheekiest gang of lascars I
ever did see, whom he allowed to bawl at you insolently, and, once fast, he plucked you out of your
berth as if he did not care what he smashed. Eighteen miles down the river you had to go behind him,
and then three more along the coast to where a
group of uninhabited rocky islets enclosed a sheltered anchorage. There you would have to lie at
single anchor with your naked spars showing to
seaward over these barren fragments of land scattered upon a very intensely blue sea. There was
nothing to look at besides but a bare coast, the muddy edge of the brown plain with the sinuosities of
the river you had left, traced in dull green, and the
Great Pagoda uprising lonely and massive with
shining curves and pinnacles like the gorgeous and
stony efflorescence of tropical rocks. You had
nothing to do but to wait fretfully for the balance
of your cargo, which was sent out of the river with
the greatest irregularity. And it was open to you
to console yourself with the thought that, after all,
this stage of bother meant that your departure from
these shores was indeed approaching at last.

[35]

FALK

We both had to go through that stage, Hermann and I, and there was a sort of tacit emulation between the ships as to which should be ready first. We kept on neck and neck almost to the finish, when I won the race by going personally to give notice in the forenoon; whereas Hermann, who was very slow in making up his mind to go ashore, did not get to the agents' office till late in the day. They told him there that my ship was first on turn for next morning, and I believe he told them he was in no hurry. It suited him better to go the day after.

That evening, on board the *Diana*, he sat with his plump knees well apart, staring and puffing at the curved mouthpiece of his pipe. Presently he spoke with some impatience to his niece about putting the children to bed. Mrs. Hermann, who was talking to Falk, stopped short and looked at her husband uneasily, but the girl got up at once and drove the children before her into the cabin. In a little while Mrs. Hermann had to leave us to quell what, from the sounds inside, must have been a dangerous mutiny. At this Hermann grumbled to himself. For half an hour longer Falk left alone with us fidgeted on his chair, sighed lightly, then at last, after drawing his hands down his face, got up, and as if renouncing the hope of making himself understood (he hadn't opened his mouth once) he said in English: " Well. . . . Good night, Captain Hermann." He stopped for a moment before my chair and looked down fixedly; I may even say he glared: and he went so far as to make a deep noise in his throat. There was in all this something so marked that for the first time in our limited intercourse of nods and grunts he excited in me something like interest. But next moment he disappointed me— for he strode away hastily without a nod even.

His manner was usually odd it is true, and I certainly did not pay much attention to it; but that sort of obscure intention, which seemed to lurk in his nonchalance like a wary old carp in a pond, had never before come so near the surface. He had distinctly aroused my expectations. I would have been unable to say what it was I expected, but at all events I did not expect the absurd developments he sprung upon me no later than the break of the very next day.

I remember only that there was, on that evening, enough point in his behaviour to make me, after he had fled, wonder audibly what he might mean. To this Hermann, crossing his legs with a swing and settling himself viciously away from me in his chair, said: " That fellow don't know himself what he means."

There might have been some insight in such a remark. I said nothing, and, still averted, he added: " When I was here last year he was just the same." An eruption of tobacco smoke enveloped his head as if his temper had exploded like gunpowder.

I had half a mind to ask him point blank whether he, at least, didn't know why Falk, a notoriously unsociable man, had taken to visiting his ship with such assiduity. After all, I reflected suddenly, it was a most remarkable thing. I wonder now what Hermann would have said. As it turned out he didn't let me ask. Forgetting all about Falk apparently, he started a monologue on his plans for the future: the selling of the ship, the going home; and falling into a reflective and calculating mood he mumbled between regular jets of smoke about the expense. The necessity of disbursing passage money for all his tribe seemed to disturb him in a manner that was the more striking because otherwise he gave no signs of a miserly disposition. And yet he fussed over the prospect of that voyage home in a mail boat like a sedentary grocer who has made up his mind to see the world. He was racially thrifty I suppose, and for him there must have been a great novelty in finding himself obliged to pay for travelling—for sea travelling which was the normal state of life for the family—from the very cradle for most of them. I could see he grudged prospectively every single shilling which must be spent so absurdly. It was rather funny. He would become doleful over it, and then again, with a fretful sigh, he would suppose there was nothing for it now but to take three second-class tickets—and there were the four children to pay for besides. A lot of money that to spend at once. A big lot of money.

I sat with him listening (not for the first time) to these heart-searchings till I grew thoroughly sleepy, and then I left him and turned in on board my ship. At daylight I was awakened by a yelping of shrill voices, accompanied by a great commotion in the water, and the short, bullying blasts of a steam-whistle. Falk with his tug had come for me.

I began to dress. It was remarkable that the answering noise on board my ship together with the patter of feet above my head ceased suddenly. But I heard more remote guttural cries which seemed to express surprise and annoyance. Then the voice of my mate reached me howling expostulations to somebody at a distance. Other voices joined, apparently indignant; a chorus of something that sounded like abuse replied. Now and then the steam-whistle screeched.

Altogether that unnecessary uproar was distracting, but down there in my cabin I took it calmly. In another moment, I thought, I should be going down that wretched river, and in another week at the most I should be totally quit of the odious place and all the odious people in it.

Greatly cheered by the idea, I seized the hair-brushes and looking at myself in the glass began to use them. Suddenly a hush fell upon the noise outside, and I heard (the ports of my cabin were thrown open)—I heard a deep calm voice, not on board my ship, however, hailing resolutely in English, but with a strong foreign twang, "Go ahead!"

There may be tides in the affairs of men which

taken at the flood . . . and so on. Personally I am still on the look out for that important turn. I am, however, afraid that most of us are fated to flounder for ever in the dead water of a pool whose shores are arid indeed. But I know that there are often in men's affairs unexpectedly—even irrationally—illuminating moments when an otherwise insignificant sound, perhaps only some perfectly commonplace gesture, suffices to reveal to us all the unreason, all the fatuous unreason, of our complacency. " Go ahead " are not particularly striking words even when pronounced with a foreign accent; yet they petrified me in the very act of smiling at myself in the glass. And then, refusing to believe my ears, but already boiling with indignation, I ran out of the cabin and up on deck.

It was incredibly true. It was perfectly true. I had no eyes for anything but the *Diana*. It was she, then, was being taken away. She was already out of her berth and shooting athwart the river. " The way this loonatic plucked that ship out is a caution," said the awed voice of my mate close to my ear. " Hey! Hallo! Falk! Hermann! What's this infernal trick? " I yelled in a fury.

Nobody heard me. Falk certainly could not hear me. His tug was turning at full speed away under the other bank. The wire hawser between her and the *Diana*, stretched as taut as a harpstring, vibrated alarmingly.

The high black craft careened over to the awful strain. A loud crack came out of her, followed by the tearing and splintering of wood. " There! " said the awed voice in my ear. " He's carried away their towing chock." And then, with enthusiasm, " Oh! Look! Look! sir, Look! at them Dutchmen skipping out of the way on the forecastle. I hope to goodness he'll break a few of their shins before he's done with 'em."

I yelled my vain protests. The rays of the rising sun coursing level along the plain warmed my back, but I was hot enough with rage. I could not have believed that a simple towing operation could suggest so plainly the idea of abduction, of rape. Falk was simply running off with the *Diana*.

The white tug careered out into the middle of the river. The red floats of her paddle-wheels revolving with mad rapidity tore up the whole reach into foam. The *Diana* in mid-stream waltzed round with as much grace as an old barn, and flew after her ravisher. Through the ragged fog of smoke driving headlong upon the water I had a glimpse of Falk's square motionless shoulders under a white hat as big as a cart-wheel, of his red face, his yellow staring eyes, his great beard. Instead of keeping a lookout ahead, he was deliberately turning his back on the river to glare at his tow. The tall heavy craft, never so used before in her life, seemed to have lost her senses; she took a wild sheer against her helm, and for a moment came straight at us, menacing and clumsy, like a runaway mountain. She piled up a streaming, hissing, boiling wave half-way up her blunt stem, my crew let out one great howl,—and then we held our breaths. It was a near thing. But Falk had her! He had her in his clutch. I fancied I could hear the steel hawser ping as it surged across the *Diana's* forecastle, with the hands on board of her bolting away from it in all directions. It was a near thing. Hermann, with his hair rumpled, in a snuffy flannel shirt and a pair of mustard-coloured trousers, had rushed to help with the wheel. I saw his terrified round face; I saw his very teeth uncovered by a sort of ghastly fixed grin; and in a great leaping tumult of water between the two ships the *Diana* whisked past so close that I could have flung a hair-brush at his head, for, it seems, I had kept them in my hands all the time. Meanwhile Mrs. Hermann sat placidly on the skylight, with a woollen shawl on her shoulders. The excellent woman in response to my indignant gesticulations fluttered a handkerchief, nodding and smiling in the kindest way imaginable. The boys, only half-dressed, were jumping about the poop in great glee, displaying their gaudy braces; and Lena in a short scarlet petticoat, with peaked elbows and thin bare arms, nursed the rag-doll with devotion. The whole family passed before my sight as if dragged across a scene of unparalleled violence. The last I saw was Hermann's niece with the baby Hermann in her arms standing apart from the others. Magnificent in her close-fitting print frock she displayed something so commanding in the manifest perfection of her figure that the sun seemed to be rising for her alone. The flood of light brought out the opulence of her form and the vigour of her youth in a glorifying way. She went by perfectly motionless and as if lost in

[44]

meditation; only the hem of her skirt stirred in the draught; the sun rays broke on her sleek tawny hair; that bald-headed ruffian, Nicholas, was whacking her on the shoulder. I saw his tiny fat arm rise and fall in a workmanlike manner. And then the four cottage windows of the *Diana* came into view retreating swiftly down the river. The sashes were up, and one of the white calico curtains was fluttered straight out like a streamer above the agitated water of the wake.

To be thus tricked out of one's turn was an unheard of occurrence. In my agent's office, where I went to complain at once, they protested with apologies they couldn't understand how the mistake arose: but Schomberg when I dropped in later to get some tiffin, though surprised to see me, was perfectly ready with an explanation. I found him seated at the end of a long narrow table, facing his wife—a scraggy little woman, with long ringlets and a blue tooth, who smiled abroad stupidly and looked frightened when you spoke to her. Between them a waggling punkah fanned twenty cane-bottomed chairs and two rows of shiny plates. Three Chinamen in white jackets loafed with napkins in their hands around that desolation. Schomberg's pet *table d'hôte* was not much of a success that day. He was feeding himself ferociously and seemed to overflow with bitterness.

He began by ordering in a brutal voice the chops to be brought back for me, and turning in his chair: "Mistake they told you? Not a bit of it! Don't you believe it for a moment, captain! Falk isn't a man to make mistakes unless on purpose." His firm conviction was that Falk had been trying all along to curry favour on the cheap with Hermann. "On the cheap—mind you! It doesn't cost him a cent to put that insult upon you, and Captain Hermann gets in a day ahead of your ship. Time's money! Eh? You are very friendly with Captain Hermann I believe, but a man is bound to be pleased at any little advantage he may get. Captain Hermann is a good business man, and there's no such thing as a friend in business. Is there?" He leaned forward and began to cast stealthy glances as usual. "But Falk is, and always was, a miserable fellow. I would despise him."

I muttered, grumpily, that I had no particular respect for Falk.

[46]

" I would despise him," he insisted, with an appearance of anxiety which would have amused me if I had not been fathoms deep in discontent. To a young man fairly conscientious and as well-meaning as only the young man can be, the current ill-usage of life comes with a peculiar cruelty. Youth that is fresh enough to believe in guilt, in innocence, and in itself, will always doubt whether it have not perchance deserved its fate. Sombre of mind and without appetite, I struggled with the chop while Mrs. Schomberg sat with her everlasting stupid grin and Schomberg's talk gathered way like a slide of rubbish.

" Let me tell you. It's all about that girl. I don't know what Captain Hermann expects, but if he asked me I could tell him something about Falk. He's a miserable fellow. That man is a perfect slave. That's what I call him. A slave. Last year I started this *table d'hôte*, and sent cards out —you know. You think he had one meal in the house? Give the thing a trial? Not once. He has got hold now of a Madras cook—a blamed fraud that I hunted out of my cookhouse with a rattan. He was not fit to cook for white men. No, not for the white men's dogs either; but, see, any damned native that can boil a pot of rice is good enough for Mr. Falk. Rice and a little fish he buys for a few cents from the fishing boats outside is what he lives on. You would hardly credit it—eh? A white man, too. . . ."

He wiped his lips, using the napkin with indignation, and looking at me. It flashed through my mind in the midst of my depression that if all the meat in the town was like these *table d'hôte* chops, Falk wasn't so far wrong. I was on the point of saying this, but Schomberg's stare was intimidating. "He's a vegetarian, perhaps," I murmured instead.

"He's a miser. A miserable miser," affirmed the hotel-keeper with great force. "The meat here is not so good as at home—of course. And dear too. But look at me. I only charge a dollar for the tiffin, and one dollar and fifty cents for the dinner. Show me anything cheaper. Why am I doing it? There's little profit in this game. Falk wouldn't look at it. I do it for the sake of a lot of young white fellows here that hadn't a place where they could get a decent meal and eat it decently in good company. There's first-rate company always at my table."

The convinced way he surveyed the empty chairs made me feel as if I had intruded upon a tiffin of ghostly Presences.

" A white man should eat like a white man, dash it all," he burst out impetuously. " Ought to eat meat, must eat meat. I manage to get meat for my patrons all the year round. Don't I? I am not catering for a dam' lot of coolies: Have another chop, captain. . . . No? You, boy—take away ! "

He threw himself back and waited grimly for the curry. The half-closed jalousies darkened the room pervaded by the smell of fresh whitewash: a swarm of flies buzzed and settled in turns, and poor Mrs. Schomberg's smile seemed to express the quintessence of all the imbecility that had ever spoken, had ever breathed, had ever been fed on infamous buffalo meat within these bare walls. Schomberg did not open his lips till he was ready to thrust therein a spoonful of greasy rice. He rolled his eyes ridiculously before he swallowed the hot stuff, and only then broke out afresh.

" It is the most degrading thing. They take the

dish up to the wheelhouse for him with a cover on it, and he shuts both the doors before he begins to eat. Fact! Must be ashamed of himself. Ask the engineer. He can't do without an engineer—don't you see—and as no respectable man can be expected to put up with such a table, he allows them fifteen dollars a month extra mess money. I assure you it is so! You just ask Mr. Ferdinand da Costa. That's the engineer he has now. You may have seen him about my place, a delicate dark young man, with very fine eyes and a little moustache. He arrived here a year ago from Calcutta. Between you and me, I guess the money-lenders there must have been after him. He rushes here for a meal every chance he can get, for just please tell me what satisfaction is that for a well-educated young fellow to feed all alone in his cabin—like a wild beast? That's what Falk expects his engineers to put up with for fifteen dollars extra. And the rows on board every time a little smell of cooking gets about the deck! You wouldn't believe! The other day da Costa got the cook to fry a steak for him—a turtle steak it was too, not beef at all—and the fat caught or something. Young da Costa himself was telling me of

it here in this room. ' Mr. Schomberg '—says he—
' if I had let a cylinder cover blow off through the
skylight by my negligence Captain Falk couldn't
have been more savage. He frightened the cook so
that he won't put anything on the fire for me now.'
Poor da Costa had tears in his eyes. Only try to
put yourself in his place, captain: a sensitive, gen-
tlemanly young fellow. Is he expected to eat his
food raw? But that's your Falk all over. Ask any
one you like. I suppose the fifteen dollars extra he
has to give keep on rankling—in there."

And Schomberg tapped his manly breast. I sat
half stunned by his irrelevant babble. Suddenly
he gripped my forearm in an impressive and cautious manner, as if to lead me into a very cavern of
confidence.

"It's nothing but enviousness," he said in a lowered tone, which had a stimulating effect upon my
wearied hearing. "I don't suppose there is one
person in this town that he isn't envious of. I tell
you he's dangerous. Even I myself am not safe
from him. I know for certain he tried to poi-
son . . . ."

"Oh, come now," I cried, revolted.

FALK

" But I know for certain. The people themselves came and told me of it. He went about saying everywhere I was a worse pest to this town than the cholera. He had been talking against me ever since I opened this hotel. And he poisoned Captain Hermann's mind too. Last time the *Diana* was loading here Captain Hermann used to come in every day for a drink or a cigar. This time he hasn't been here twice in a week. How do you account for that?"

He squeezed my arm till he extorted from me some sort of mumble.

" He makes ten times the money I do. I've another hotel to fight against, and there is no other tug on the river. I am not in his way, am I? He wouldn't be fit to run an hotel if he tried. But that's just his nature. He can't bear to think I am making a living. I only hope it makes him properly wretched. He's like that in everything. He would like to keep a decent table well enough. But no—for the sake of a few cents. Can't do it. It's too much for him. That's what I call being a slave to it. But he's mean enough to kick up a row when his nose gets tickled a bit. See that? That just paints him. Miserly and envious. You can't account for it any other way. Can you? I have been studying him these three years."

He was anxious I should assent to his theory. And indeed on thinking it over it would have been plausible enough if there hadn't been always the essential falseness of irresponsibility in Schomberg's chatter. However, I was not disposed to investigate the psychology of Falk. I was engaged just then in eating despondently a piece of stale Dutch cheese, being too much crushed to care what I swallowed myself, let alone bothering my head about Falk's ideas of gastronomy. I could expect from their study no clue to his conduct in matters of business, which seemed to me totally unrestrained by morality or even by the commonest sort of decency. How insignificant and contemptible I must appear, for the fellow to dare treat me like this—I reflected suddenly, writhing in silent agony. And I consigned Falk and all his peculiarities to the devil with so much mental fervour as to forget Schomberg's existence, till he grabbed my arm urgently. "Well, you may think and think till every hair of your head falls off, captain; but you can't explain it in any other way."

[53]

For the sake of peace and quietness I admitted hurriedly that I couldn't; persuaded that now he would leave off. But the only result was to make his moist face shine with the pride of cunning. He removed his hand for a moment to scare a black mass of flies off the sugar-basin and caught hold of my arm again.

"To be sure. And in the same way everybody is aware he would like to get married. Only he can't. Let me quote you an instance. Well, two years ago a Miss Vanlo, a very ladylike girl, came from home to keep house for her brother, Fred, who had an engineering shop for small repairs by the water side. Suddenly Falk takes to going up to their bungalow after dinner, and sitting for hours in the verandah saying nothing. The poor girl couldn't tell for the life of her what to do with such a man, so she would keep on playing the piano and singing to him evening after evening till she was ready to drop. And it wasn't as if she had been a strong young woman either. She was thirty, and the climate had been playing the deuce with her. Then—don't you know—Fred had to sit up with them for propriety, and during whole weeks on end never got

[54]

FALK

a single chance to get to bed before midnight.
That was not pleasant for a tired man—was it?
And besides Fred had worries then because his shop
didn't pay and he was dropping money fast. He
just longed to get away from here and try his luck
somewhere else, but for the sake of his sister he
hung on and on till he ran himself into debt over his
ears—I can tell you. I, myself, could show a hand-
ful of his chits for meals and drinks in my drawer.
I could never find out tho' where he found all the
money at last. Can't be but he must have got something out of that brother of his, a coal merchant in
Port Said. Anyhow he paid everybody before he
left, but the girl nearly broke her heart. Disappointment, of course, and at her age, don't you
know.... Mrs. Schomberg here was very friendly
with her, and she could tell you. Awful despair.
Fainting fits. It was a scandal. A notorious scandal. To that extent that old Mr. Siegers—not
your present charterer, but Mr. Siegers the father,
the old gentleman who retired from business on a
fortune and got buried at sea going home, *he* had
to interview Falk in his private office. He was a
man who could speak like a Dutch Uncle, and, be-

[55]

sides, Messrs. Siegers had been helping Falk with a good bit of money from the start. In fact you may say they made him as far as that goes. It so happened that just at the time he turned up here, their firm was chartering a lot of sailing ships every year, and it suited their business that there should be good towing facilities on the river. See? . . . Well—there's always an ear at the keyhole— isn't there? In fact," he lowered his tone confidentially, " in this case a good friend of mine; a man you can see here any evening; only they conversed rather low. Anyhow my friend's certain that Falk was trying to make all sorts of excuses, and old Mr. Siegers was coughing a lot. And yet Falk wanted all the time to be married too. Why! It's notorious the man has been longing for years to make a home for himself. Only he can't face the expense. When it comes to putting his hand in his pocket— it chokes him off. That's the truth and no other. I've always said so, and everybody agrees with me by this time. What do you think of that—eh? "

He appealed confidently to my indignation, but having a mind to annoy him I remarked, " that it seemed to me very pitiful—if true."

FALK

He bounced in his chair as if I had run a pin into him. I don't know what he might have said, only at that moment we heard through the half open door of the billiard-room the footsteps of two men entering from the verandah, a murmur of two voices; at the sharp tapping of a coin on a table Mrs. Schomberg half rose irresolutely. " Sit still," he hissed at her, and then, in an hospitable, jovial tone, contrasting amazingly with the angry glance that had made his wife sink in her chair, he cried very loud: " Tiffin still going on in here, gentlemen."

There was no answer, but the voices dropped suddenly. The head Chinaman went out. We heard the clink of ice in the glasses, pouring sounds, the shuffling of feet, the scraping of chairs. Schomberg, after wondering in a low mutter who the devil could be there at this time of the day, got up napkin in hand to peep through the doorway cautiously. He retreated rapidly on tip-toe, and whispering behind his hand informed me that it was Falk, Falk himself who was in there, and, what's more, he had Captain Hermann with him.

The return of the tug from the outer Roads was

unexpected but possible, for Falk had taken away the *Diana* at half-past five, and it was now two o'clock. Schomberg wished me to observe that neither of these men would spend a dollar on a tiffin, which they must have wanted. But by the time I was ready to leave the dining-room Falk had gone. I heard the last of his big boots on the planks of the verandah. Hermann was sitting quite alone in the large, wooden room with the two lifeless billiard tables shrouded in striped covers, mopping his face diligently. He wore his best go-ashore clothes, a stiff collar, black coat, large white waistcoat, grey trousers. A white cotton sunshade with a cane handle reposed between his legs, his side whiskers were neatly brushed, his chin had been freshly shaved; and he only distantly resembled the dishevelled and terrified man in a snuffy night shirt and ignoble old trousers I had seen in the morning hanging on to the wheel of the *Diana*.

He gave a start at my entrance, and addressed me at once in some confusion, but with genuine eagerness. He was anxious to make it clear he had nothing to do with what he called the " tam pizness " of the morning. It was most inconvenient.

He had reckoned upon another day up in town to settle his bills and sign certain papers. There were also some few stores to come, and sundry pieces of " my ironwork," as he called it quaintly, landed for repairs, had been left behind. Now he would have to hire a native boat to take all this out to the ship. It would cost five or six dollars perhaps. He had had no warning from Falk. Nothing. . . . He hit the table with his dumpy fist. . . . Der verfluchte Kerl came in the morning like a " tam' ropper," making a great noise, and took him away. His mate was not prepared, his ship was moored fast—he protested it was shameful to come upon a man in that way. Shameful! Yet such was the power Falk had on the river that when I suggested in a chilling tone that he might have simply refused to have his ship moved, Hermann was quite startled at the idea. I never realised so well before that this is an age of steam. The exclusive possession of a marine boiler had given Falk the whiphand of us all. Hermann, recovering, put it to me appealingly that I knew very well how unsafe it was to contradict that fellow. At this I only smiled distantly.

" Der Kerl! " he cried. He was sorry he had not

refused. He was indeed. The damage! The damage! What for all that damage! There was no occasion for damage. Did I know how much damage he had done? It gave me a certain satisfaction to tell him that I had heard his old waggon of a ship crack fore and aft as she went by. "You passed close enough to me," I added significantly.

He threw both his hands up to heaven at the recollection. One of them grasped by the middle the white parasol, and he resembled curiously a caricature of a shopkeeping citizen in one of his own German comic papers. "Ach! That was dangerous," he cried. I was amused. But directly he added with an appearance of simplicity, "The side of your iron ship would have been crushed in like— like this matchbox."

"Would it?" I growled, much less amused now; but by the time I had decided that this remark was not meant for a dig at me he had worked himself into a high state of resentfulness against Falk. The inconvenience, the damage, the expense! Gottferdam! Devil take the fellow. Behind the bar Schomberg with a cigar in his teeth, pretended to be writing with a pencil on a large sheet of paper;

[60]

and as Hermann's excitement increased it made me comfortingly aware of my own calmness and superiority. But it occurred to me while I listened to his revilings, that after all the good man had come up in the tug. There perhaps—since he must come to town—he had no option. But evidently he had had a drink with Falk, either accepted or offered. How was that? So I checked him by saying loftily that I hoped he would make Falk pay for every penny of the damage.

" That's it! That's it! Go for him," called out Schomberg from the bar, flinging his pencil down and rubbing his hands.

We ignored his noise. But Hermann's excitement suddenly went off the boil as when you remove a saucepan from the fire. I urged on his consideration that he had done now with Falk and Falk's confounded tug. He, Hermann, would not, perhaps, turn up again in this part of the world for years to come, since he was going to sell the *Diana* at the end of this very trip (" Go home passenger in a mail boat," he murmured mechanically). He was therefore safe from Falk's malice. All he had to do was to race off to his consignees and stop payment of the towage bill before Falk had the time to get in and lift the money.

Nothing could have been less in the spirit of my advice than the thoughtful way in which he set about to make his parasol stay propped against the edge of the table.

While I watched his concentrated efforts with astonishment he threw at me one or two perplexed, half-shy glances. Then he sat down. "That's all very well," he said reflectively.

It cannot be doubted that the man had been thrown off his balance by being hauled out of the harbour against his wish. His stolidity had been profoundly stirred, else he would never have made up his mind to ask me unexpectedly whether I had not remarked that Falk had been casting eyes upon his niece. "No more than myself," I answered with literal truth. The girl was of the sort one necessarily casts eyes at in a sense. She made no noise, but she filled most satisfactorily a good bit of space.

"But you, captain, are not the same kind of man," observed Hermann.

I was not, I am happy to say, in a position to deny this. "What about the lady?" I could not help asking. At this he gazed for a time into my face, earnestly, and made as if to change the subject. I heard him beginning to mutter something unexpected, about his children growing old enough to require schooling. He would have to leave them ashore with their grandmother when he took up that new command he expected to get in Germany.

This constant harping on his domestic arrangements was funny. I suppose it must have been like the prospect of a complete alteration in his life. An epoch. He was going, too, to part with the *Diana!* He had served in her for years. He had inherited her. From an uncle, if I remember rightly. And the future loomed big before him, occupying his thought exclusively with all its aspects as on the eve of a venturesome enterprise. He sat there frowning and biting his lip, and suddenly he began to fume and fret.

I discovered to my momentary amusement that he seemed to imagine I could, should or ought, have caused Falk in some way to pronounce himself. Such a hope was incomprehensible, but funny. Then the contact with all this foolishness irritated me. I said crossly that I had seen no symptoms,

but if there were any —since he, Hermann, was so
sure—then it was still worse. What pleasure Falk
found in humbugging people in just that way I
couldn't say. It was, however, my solemn duty to
warn him. It had lately, I said, come to my knowledge that there was a man (not a very long time
ago either) who had been taken in just like this.

All this passed in undertones, and at this point
Schomberg, exasperated at our secrecy, went out
of the room slamming the door with a crash that
positively lifted us in our chairs. This, or else what
I had said, huffed my Hermann. He supposed, with
a contemptuous toss of his head towards the door
which trembled yet, that I had got hold of some of
that man's silly tales. It looked, indeed, as though
his mind had been thoroughly poisoned against
Schomberg. " His tales were—they were," he repeated, seeking for the word—" trash." They
were trash, he reiterated, and moreover I was young
yet . . .

This horrid aspersion (I regret I am no longer
exposed to that sort of insult) made me huffy too.
I felt ready in my own mind to back up every asser-
tion of Schomberg's and on any subject. In a mo-

ment, devil only knows why, Hermann and I were looking at each other most inimically. He caught up his hat without more ado and I gave myself the pleasure of calling after him:

"Take my advice and make Falk pay for breaking up your ship. You aren't likely to get anything else out of him."

When I got on board my ship later on, the old mate, who was very full of the events of the morning, remarked:

"I saw the tug coming back from the outer Roads just before two P.M." (He never by any chance used the words morning or afternoon. Always P.M. or A.M., log-book style.) "Smart work that. Man's always in a state of hurry. He's a regular chucker-out, ain't he, sir? There's a few pubs I know of in the East-end of London that would be all the better for one of his sort around the bar." He chuckled at his joke. "A regular chucker-out. Now he has fired out that Dutchman head over heels, I suppose our turn's coming to-morrow morning."

We were all on deck at break of day (even the sick—poor devils—had crawled out) ready to cast off in the twinkling of an eye. Nothing came.

Falk did not come. At last, when I began to think that probably something had gone wrong in his engine-room, we perceived the tug going by, full pelt, down the river, as if we hadn't existed. For a moment I entertained the wild notion that he was going to turn round in the next reach. Afterwards I watched his smoke appear above the plain, now here, now there, according to the windings of the river. It disappeared. Then without a word I went down to breakfast. I just simply went down to breakfast.

Not one of us uttered a sound till the mate, after imbibing—by means of suction out of a saucer—his second cup of tea, exclaimed: "Where the devil is the man gone to?"

"Courting!" I shouted, with such a fiendish laugh that the old chap didn't venture to open his lips any more.

I started to the office perfectly calm. Calm with excessive rage. Evidently they knew all about it already, and they treated me to a show of consternation. The manager, a soft-footed, immensely obese man, breathing short, got up to meet me, while all round the room the young clerks, bending over the papers on their desks, cast upward glances in my direction. The fat man, without waiting for my complaint, wheezing heavily and in a tone as if he himself were incredulous, conveyed to me the news that Falk—Captain Falk— had declined—had absolutely declined—to tow my ship—to have anything to do with my ship—this day or any other day. Never!

I did my best to preserve a cool appearance, but, all the same, I must have shown how much taken aback I was. We were talking in the middle of the room. Suddenly behind my back some ass blew his nose with great force, and at the same time another quill-driver jumped up and went out on the landing hastily. It occurred to me I was cutting a foolish figure there. I demanded angrily to see the principal in his private room.

The skin of Mr. Siegers' head showed dead white between the iron grey streaks of hair lying plastered cross-wise from ear to ear over the top of his skull in the manner of a bandage. His narrow sunken face was of an uniform and permanent terra-cotta colour, like a piece of pottery. He was sickly, thin, and short, with wrists like a boy of ten.

[67]

But from that debile body there issued a bullying voice, tremendously loud, harsh and resonant, as if produced by some powerful mechanical contrivance in the nature of a fog-horn. I do not know what he did with it in the private life of his home, but in the larger sphere of business it presented the advantage of overcoming arguments without the slightest mental effort, by the mere volume of sound. We had had several passages of arms. It took me all I knew to guard the interests of my owners—whom, *nota bene*, I had never seen—while Siegers (who had made their acquaintance some years before, during a business tour in Australia) pretended to the knowledge of their innermost minds, and, in the character of " our very good friends," threw them perpetually at my head.

He looked at me with a jaundiced eye (there was no love lost between us), and declared at once that it was strange, very strange. His pronunciation of English was so extravagant that I can't even attempt to reproduce it. For instance, he said " Fferie strantch." Combined with the bellowing intonation it made the language of one's childhood sound weirdly startling, and even if considered purely as a kind of unmeaning noise it filled you with astonishment at first. " They had," he continued, " been acquainted with Captain Falk for very many years, and never had any reason. . . ."

" That's why I come to you, of course," I interrupted. " I've the right to know the meaning of this infernal nonsense." In the half light of the room, which was greenish, because of the tree-tops screening the window, I saw him writhe his meagre shoulders. It came into my head, as disconnected ideas will come at all sorts of times into one's head, that this, most likely, was the very room where, if the tale were true, Falk had been lectured by Mr. Siegers, the father. Mr. Siegers' (the son's) overwhelming voice, in brassy blasts, as though he had been trying to articulate his words through a trombone, was expressing his great regret at a conduct characterised by a very marked want of discretion. . . As I lived I was being lectured too ! His deafening gibberish was difficult to follow, but it was *my* conduct—mine!—that . . . Damn! I wasn't going to stand this.

" What on earth are you driving at? " I asked in a passion. I put my hat on my head (he never

offered a seat to anybody), and as he seemed for
the moment struck dumb by my irreverence, I
turned my back on him and marched out. His vo-
cal arrangements blared after me a few threats of
coming down on the ship for the demurrage of the
lighters, and all the other expenses consequent
upon the delays arising from my frivolity.

Once outside in the sunshine my head swam. It
was no longer a question of mere delay. I perceived myself involved in hopeless and humiliating
absurdities that were leading me to something very
like a disaster. " Let us be calm," I muttered to
myself, and ran into the shade of a leprous wall.
From that short side-street I could see the broad
main thoroughfare ruinous and gay, running
away, away between stretches of decaying mason-
ry, bamboo fences, ranges of arcades of brick and
plaster, hovels of lath and mud, lofty temple gates
of carved timber, huts of rotten mats—an immensely wide thoroughfare, loosely packed as far
as the eye could reach with a barefooted and brown
multitude paddling ankle deep in the dust. For a
moment I felt myself about to go out of my mind
with worry and desperation.

FALK

Some allowance must be made for the feelings of a young man new to responsibility. I thought of my crew. Half of them were ill, and I really began to think that some of them would end by dying on board if I couldn't get them out to sea soon. Obviously I should have to take my ship down the river, either working under canvas or dredging with the anchor down; operations which, in common with many modern sailors, I only knew theoretically. And I almost shrank from undertaking them shorthanded and without local knowledge of the river bed, which is so necessary for the confident handling of the ship. There were no pilots, no beacons, no buoys of any sort; but there was a very devil of a current for anybody to see, no end of shoal places, and at least two obviously awkward turns of the channel between me and the sea. But how dangerous these turns were I would not tell. I didn't even know what my ship was capable of! I had never handled her in my life. A misunderstanding between a man and his ship in a difficult river with no room to make it up, is bound to end in trouble for the man. On the other hand, it must be owned I had not much reason to count upon a

[71]

general run of good luck. And suppose I had the misfortune to pile her up high and dry on some beastly shoal? That would have been the final undoing of that voyage. It was plain that if Falk refused to tow me out he would also refuse to pull me off. This meant—what? A day lost at the very best; but more likely a whole fortnight of frizzling on some pestilential mudflat, of desperate work, of discharging cargo; more than likely it meant borrowing money at an exorbitant rate of interest—from the Siegers' gang too at that. They were a power in the port. And that elderly seaman of mine, Gambril, had looked pretty ghastly when I went forward to dose him with quinine that morning. *He* would certainly die—not to speak of two or three others that seemed nearly as bad, and of the rest of them just ready to catch any tropical disease going. Horror, ruin and everlasting remorse. And no help. None. I had fallen amongst a lot of unfriendly lunatics!

At any rate, if I must take my ship down myself it was my duty to procure if possible some local knowledge. But that was not easy. The only person I could think of for that service was a certain

FALK

Johnson, formerly captain of a country ship, but now spliced to a country wife and gone utterly to the bad. I had only heard of him in the vaguest way, as living concealed in the thick of two hundred thousand natives, and only emerging into the light of day for the purpose of hunting up some brandy. I had a notion that if I could lay my hands on him I would sober him on board my ship and use him for a pilot. Better than nothing. Once a sailor always a sailor—and he had known the river for years. But in our Consulate (where I arrived dripping after a sharp walk) they could tell me nothing. The excellent young men on the staff, though willing to help me, belonged to a sphere of the white colony for which that sort of Johnson does not exist. Their suggestion was that I should hunt the man up myself with the help of the Consulate's constable—an ex-sergeant-major of a regiment of Hussars.

This man, whose usual duty apparently consisted in sitting behind a little table in an outer room of Consular offices, when ordered to assist me in my search for Johnson displayed lots of energy and a marvellous amount of local knowledge of a

FALK

sort. But he did not conceal an immense and sceptical contempt for the whole business. We explored together on that afternoon an infinity of infamous grog shops, gambling dens, opium dens. We walked up narrow lanes where our gharry—a tiny box of a thing on wheels, attached to a jibbing Burmah pony—could by no means have passed. The constable seemed to be on terms of scornful intimacy with Maltese, with Eurasians, with Chinamen, with Klings, and with the sweepers attached to a temple, with whom he talked at the gate. We interviewed also through a grating in a mud wall closing a blind alley an immensely corpulent Italian, who, the ex-sergeant-major remarked to me perfunctorily, had " killed another man last year." Thereupon he addressed him as " Antonio " and " Old Buck," though that bloated carcase, apparently more than half filling the sort of cell wherein it sat, recalled rather a fat pig in a stye. Familiar and never unbending, the sergeant chucked —absolutely chucked—under the chin a horribly wrinkled and shrivelled old hag propped on a stick, who had volunteered some sort of information: and with the same stolid face he kept up an animated conversation with the groups of swathed brown women, who sat smoking cheroots on the door-steps of a long range of clay hovels. We got out of the gharry and clambered into dwellings airy like packing crates, or descended into places sinister like cellars. We got in, we drove on, we got out again for the sole purpose, as it seemed, of looking behind a heap of rubble. The sun declined; my companion was curt and sardonic in his answers, but it appears we were just missing Johnson all along. At last our conveyance stopped once more with a jerk, and the driver jumping down opened the door.

A black mudhole blocked the lane. A mound of garbage crowned with the dead body of a dog arrested us not. An empty Australian beef tin bounded cheerily before the toe of my boot. Suddenly we clambered through a gap in a prickly fence. . . .

It was a very clean native compound: and the big native woman, with bare brown legs as thick as bedposts, pursuing on all fours a silver dollar that came rolling out from somewhere, was Mrs. Johnson herself. " Your man's at home," said the

ex-sergeant, and stepped aside in complete and
marked indifference to anything that might follow.
Johnson—at home—stood with his back to a native
house built on posts and with its walls made of
mats. In his left hand he held a banana. Out of
the right he dealt another dollar into space. The
woman captured this one on the wing, and there
and then plumped down on the ground to look at
us with greater comfort.

My man was sallow of face, grizzled, unshaven,
muddy on elbows and back; where the seams of his
serge coat yawned you could see his white naked-
ness. The vestiges of a paper collar encircled his
neck. He looked at us with a grave, swaying surprise. "Where do you come from?" he asked.
My heart sank. How could I have been stupid
enough to waste energy and time for this?

But having already gone so far I approached a
little nearer and declared the purpose of my visit.
He would have to come at once with me, sleep on
board my ship, and to-morrow, with the first of the
ebb, he would give me his assistance in getting my
ship down to the sea, without steam. A six-hun-
dred-ton barque, drawing nine feet aft. I pro-

posed to give him eighteen dollars for his local
knowledge; and all the time I was speaking he
kept on considering attentively the various aspects
of the banana, holding first one side up to his eye,
then the other.

" You've forgotten to apologise," he said at last
with extreme precision. " Not being a gentleman
yourself, you don't know apparently when you in-
trude upon a gentleman. I am one. I wish you to
understand that when I am in funds I don't work,
and now . . ."

I would have pronounced him perfectly sober
hadn't he paused in great concern to try and brush
a hole off the knee of his trousers.

" I have money—and friends. Every gentleman has. Perhaps you would like to know my
friend? His name is Falk. You could borrow
some money. Try to remember. F-A-L-K, Falk."
Abruptly his tone changed. " A noble heart," he
said muzzily.

" Has Falk been giving you some money? " I
asked, appalled by the detailed finish of the dark
plot.

" Lent me, my good man, not given me. Lent,"

he corrected suavely. " Met me taking the air last evening, and being as usual anxious to oblige —— Hadn't you better go to the devil out of my compound? "

And upon this, without other warning, he let fly with the banana which missed my head, and took the constable just under the left eye. He rushed at the miserable Johnson, stammering with fury. They fell. . . . But why dwell on the wretchedness, the breathlessness, the degradation, the senselessness, the weariness, the ridicule and humiliation and—and—the perspiration, of these moments? I dragged the ex-hussar off. He was like a wild beast. It seems he had been greatly annoyed at losing his free afternoon on my account. The garden of his bungalow required his personal attention, and at the slight blow of the banana the brute in him had broken loose. We left Johnson on his back, still black in the face, but beginning to kick feebly. Meantime, the big woman had remained sitting on the ground, apparently paralysed with extreme terror.

For half an hour we jolted inside our rolling box, side by side, in profound silence. The ex-ser-

geant was busy staunching the blood of a long
scratch on his cheek. " I hope you're satisfied," he
said suddenly. " That's what comes of all that
tomfool business. If you hadn't quarrelled with
that tugboat skipper over some girl or other, all
this wouldn't have happened."

" You heard *that* story?" I said.

" Of course I heard. And I shouldn't wonder if
the Consul-General himself doesn't come to hear
of it. How am I to go before him to-morrow with
that thing on my cheek—I want to know. Its
you who ought to have got this!"

After that, till the gharry stopped and he
jumped out without leave-taking, he swore to himself steadily, horribly; muttering great, purpose-
ful, trooper oaths, to which the worst a sailor can
do is like the prattle of a child. For my part I had
just the strength to crawl into Schomberg's coffee-
room, where I wrote at a little table a note to the
mate instructing him to get everything ready for
dropping down the river next day. I couldn't
face my ship. Well! she had a clever sort of skipper and no mistake—poor thing! What a horrid
mess! I took my head between my hands. At

times the obviousness of my innocence would reduce
me to despair. What had I done? If I had done
something to bring about the situation I should at
least have learned not to do it again. But I felt
guiltless to the point of imbecility. The room was
empty yet; only Schomberg prowled round me
goggle-eyed and with a sort of awed respectful curiosity. No doubt he had set the story going himself; but he was a good-hearted chap, and I am
really persuaded he participated in all my troubles.
He did what he could for me. He ranged aside the
heavy matchstand, set a chair straight, pushed a
spittoon slightly with his foot—as you show small
attentions to a friend under a great sorrow—
sighed, and at last, unable to hold his tongue:

"Well! I warned you, captain. That's what
comes of running your head against Mr. Falk.
Man'll stick at nothing."

I sat without stirring, and after surveying me
with a sort of commiseration in his eyes he burst
out in a hoarse whisper: "But for a fine lump of
a girl, she's a fine lump of a girl." He made a loud
smacking noise with his thick lips. "The finest
lump of a girl that I ever . . ." he was going on

with great unction, but for some reason or other broke off. I fancied myself throwing something at his head. "I don't blame you, captain. Hang me if I do," he said with a patronising air.

"Thank you," I said resignedly. It was no use fighting against this false fate. I don't know even if I was sure myself where the truth of the matter began. The conviction that it would end disastrously had been driven into me by all the successive shocks my sense of security had received. I began to ascribe an extraordinary potency to agents in themselves powerless. It was as if Schomberg's baseless gossip had the power to bring about the thing itself or the abstract enmity of Falk could put my ship ashore.

I have already explained how fatal this last would have been. For my further action, my youth, my inexperience, my very real concern for the health of my crew must be my excuse. The action itself, when it came, was purely impulsive. It was set in movement quite undiplomatically and simply by Falk's appearance in the doorway.

The room was full by then and buzzing with

voices. I had been looked at with curiosity by every one, but how am I to describe the sensation produced by the appearance of Falk himself blocking the doorway? The tension of expectation could be measured by the profundity of the silence that fell upon the very click of the billiard balls. As to Schomberg, he looked extremely frightened; he hated mortally any sort of row (*fracas* he called it) in his establishment. *Fracas* was bad for business, he affirmed; but, in truth, this specimen of portly, middle-aged manhood was of a timid disposition. I don't know what, considering my presence in the place, they all hoped would come of it. A sort of stag fight, perhaps. Or they may have supposed Falk had come in only to annihilate me completely. As a matter of fact, Falk had come in because Hermann had asked him to inquire after the precious white cotton parasol which, in the worry and excitement of the previous day, he had forgotten at the table where we had held our little discussion.

It was this that gave me my opportunity. I don't think I would have gone to seek Falk out. No. I don't think so. There are limits. But there was an opportunity and I seized it—I have already tried to explain why. Now I will merely state that, in my opinion, to get his sickly crew into the sea air and secure a quick despatch for his ship a skipper would be justified in going to any length, short of absolute crime. He should put his pride in his pocket; he may accept confidences; explain his innocence as if it were a sin; he may take advantage of misconceptions, of desires and of weaknesses; he ought to conceal his horror and other emotions, and, if the fate of a human being, and that human being a magnificent young girl, is strangely involved—why, he should contemplate that fate (whatever it might seem to be) without turning a hair. And all these things I have done; the explaining, the listening, the pretending—even to the discretion—and nobody, not even Hermann's niece, I believe, need throw stones at me now. Schomberg at all events needn't, since from first to last, I am happy to say, there was not the slightest " fracas."

Overcoming a nervous contraction of the windpipe, I had managed to exclaim " Captain Falk! " His start of surprise was perfectly genuine, but

afterwards he neither smiled nor scowled. He simply waited. Then, when I had said, " I must have
a talk with you," and had pointed to a chair at my
table, he moved up to me, though he didn't sit
down. Schomberg, however, with a long tumbler
in his hand, was making towards us prudently, and
I discovered then the only sign of weakness in Falk.
He had for Schomberg a repulsion resembling that
sort of physical fear some people experience at the
sight of a toad. Perhaps to a man so essentially
and silently concentrated upon himself (though he
could talk well enough, as I was to find out
presently) the other's irrepressible loquacity, em-
bracing every human being within range of the
tongue, might have appeared unnatural, disgust-
ing, and monstrous. He suddenly gave signs of
restiveness—positively like a horse about to rear,
and, muttering hurriedly as if in great pain, " No.
I can't stand that fellow," seemed ready to bolt.
This weakness of his gave me the advantage at the
very start. " Verandah," I suggested, as if ren-
dering him a service, and walked him out by the
arm. We stumbled over a few chairs; we had the
feeling of open space before us, and felt the fresh

breath of the river—fresh, but tainted. The Chinese theatres across the water made, in the sparsely twinkling masses of gloom an Eastern town presents at night, blazing centres of light, and of a distant and howling uproar. I felt him become suddenly tractable again like an animal, like a good-tempered horse when the object that scares him is removed. Yes. I felt in the darkness there how tractable he was, without my conviction of his inflexibility—tenacity, rather, perhaps—being in the least weakened. His very arm abandoning itself to my grasp was as hard as marble—like a limb of iron. But I heard a tumultuous scuffling of boot-soles within. The unspeakable idiots inside were crowding to the windows, climbing over each other's backs behind the blinds, billiard cues and all. Somebody broke a window pane, and with the sound of falling glass, so suggestive of riot and devastation, Schomberg reeled out after us in a state of funk which had prevented his parting with his brandy and soda. He must have trembled like an aspen leaf. The piece of ice in the long tumbler he held in his hand tinkled with an effect of chattering teeth. " I beg you, gentlemen," he expost-

ulated thickly. " Come! Really, now, I must in-
sist . . ."

How proud I am of my presence of mind!
" Hallo," I said instantly in a loud and naïve tone,
" somebody's breaking your windows, Schomberg.
Would you please tell one of your boys to bring
out here a pack of cards and a couple of lights?
And two long drinks. Will you? "

To receive an order soothed him at once. It was
business. " Certainly," he said in an immensely
relieved tone. The night was rainy, with wandering gusts of wind, and while we waited for the candles Falk said, as if to justify his panic, " I don't
interfere in anybody's business. I don't give any
occasion for talk. I am a respectable man. But
this fellow is always making out something wrong,
and can never rest till he gets somebody to believe
him."

This was the first of my knowledge of Falk.
This desire of respectability, of being like everybody else, was the only recognition he vouchsafed
to the organisation of mankind. For the rest he
might have been the member of a herd, not of a so-
ciety. Self-preservation was his only concern.

[86]

Not selfishness, but mere self-preservation. Selfishness presupposes consciousness, choice, the presence of other men; but his instinct acted as though he were the last of mankind nursing that law like the only spark of a sacred fire. I don't mean to say that living naked in a cavern would have satisfied him. Obviously he was the creature of the conditions to which he was born. No doubt self-preservation meant also the preservation of these conditions. But essentially it meant something much more simple, natural, and powerful. How shall I express it? It meant the preservation of the five senses of his body—let us say—taking it in its narrowest as well as in its widest meaning. I think you will admit before long the justice of this judgment. However, as we stood there together in the dark verandah I had judged nothing as yet—and I had no desire to judge—which is an idle practice anyhow. The light was long in coming.

"Of course," I said in a tone of mutual understanding, "it isn't exactly a game of cards I want with you."

I saw him draw his hands down his face—the

vague stir of the passionate and meaningless gesture; but he waited in silent patience. It was only
when the lights had been brought out that he
opened his lips. I understood his mumble to mean
that " he didn't know any game."

" Like this Schomberg and all the other fools
will have to keep off," I said tearing open the pack.
" Have you heard that we are universally supposed
to be quarrelling about a girl? You know who—
of course. I am really ashamed to ask, but is it
possible that you do me the honour to think me dangerous? "

As I said these words I felt how absurd it was
and also I felt flattered—for, really, what else
could it be? His answer, spoken in his usual dis-
passionate undertone, made it clear that it was so,
but not precisely as flattering as I supposed. He
thought me dangerous with Hermann, more than
with the girl herself; but, as to quarrelling, I saw
at once how inappropriate the word was. We had
no quarrel. Natural forces are not quarrelsome.
You can't quarrel with the wind that inconveniences
and humiliates you by blowing off your hat in a
street full of people. He had no quarrel with me.

FALK

Neither would a boulder, falling on my head, have
had. He fell upon me in accordance with the law
by which he was moved—not of gravitation, like a
detached stone, but of self-preservation. Of course
this is giving it a rather wide interpretation.
Strictly speaking, he had existed and could have
existed without being married. Yet he told me that
he had found it more and more difficult to live
alone. Yes. He told me this in his low, careless
voice, to such a pitch of confidence had we arrived
at the end of half an hour.

It took me just about that time to convince him
that I had never dreamed of marrying Hermann's
niece. Could any necessity have been more extravagant? And the difficulty was the greater because
he was so hard hit that he couldn't imagine anybody being able to remain in a state of indifference.
Any man with eyes in his head, he seemed to think,
could not help coveting so much bodily magnifi-
cence. This profound belief was conveyed by the
manner he listened sitting sideways to the table and
playing absently with a few cards I had dealt to
him at random. And the more I saw into him the
more I saw of him. The wind swayed the lights

so that his sunburnt face, whiskered to the eyes, seemed to successively flicker crimson at me and to go out. I saw the extraordinary breadth of the high cheek-bones, the perpendicular style of the features, the massive forehead, steep like a cliff, denuded at the top, largely uncovered at the temples. The fact is I had never before seen him without his hat; but now, as if my fervour had made him hot, he had taken it off and laid it gently on the floor. Something peculiar in the shape and setting of his yellow eyes gave them the provoking silent intensity which characterised his glance. But the face was thin, furrowed, worn; I discovered that through the bush of his hair, as you may detect the gnarled shape of a tree trunk lost in a dense undergrowth. These overgrown cheeks were sunken. It was an anchorite's bony head fitted with a Capuchin's beard and adjusted to a herculean body. I don't mean athletic. Hercules, I take it, was not an athlete. He was a strong man, susceptible to female charms, and not afraid of dirt. And thus with Falk, who was a strong man. He was extremely strong, just as the girl (since I must think of them together) was magnificently at-

tractive by the masterful power of flesh and blood,
expressed in shape, in size, in attitude—that is by
a straight appeal to the senses. His mind meantime, preoccupied with respectability, quailed before Schomberg's tongue and seemed absolutely
impervious to my protestations; and I went so far
as to protest that I would just as soon think of
marrying my mother's (dear old lady!) faithful
female cook as Hermann's niece. Sooner, I protested, in my desperation, much sooner; but it did
not appear that he saw anything outrageous in the
proposition, and in his sceptical immobility he
seemed to nurse the argument that at all events the
cook was very, very far away. It must be said that,
just before, I had gone wrong by appealing to the
evidence of my manner whenever I called on board
the *Diana*. I had never attempted to approach the
girl, or to speak to her, or even to look at her in any
marked way. Nothing could be clearer. But, as
his own idea of—let us say—courting, seemed to
consist precisely in sitting silently for hours in the
vicinity of the beloved object, that line of argument inspired him with distrust. Staring down his
extended legs he let out a grunt—as much as to

say, " That's all very fine, but you can't throw dust in *my* eyes."

At last I was exasperated into saying, " Why don't you put the matter at rest by talking to Hermann? " and I added sneeringly: " You don't expect me perhaps to speak for you? "

To this he said, very loud for him, " Would you? "

And for the first time he lifted his head to look at me with wonder and incredulity. He lifted his head so sharply that there could be no mistake. I had touched a spring. I saw the whole extent of my opportunity, and could hardly believe in it.

" Why. Speak to . . . Well, of course," I proceeded very slowly, watching him with great attention, for, on my word, I feared a joke. " Not, perhaps, to the young lady herself. I can't speak German, you know. But . . ."

He interrupted me with the earnest assurance that Hermann had the highest opinion of me; and at once I felt the need for the greatest possible diplomacy at this juncture. So I demurred just enough to draw him on. Falk sat up, but except for a very noticeable enlargement of the pupils, till the irises of his eyes were reduced to two narrow yellow rings, his face, I should judge, was incapable of expressing excitement. " Oh, yes! Hermann did have the greatest . . ."

" Take up your cards. Here's Schomberg peeping at us through the blind! " I said.

We went through the motions of what might have been a game of écarté. Presently the intolerable scandalmonger withdrew, probably to inform the people in the billiard-room that we two were gambling on the verandah like mad.

We were not gambling, but it was a game; a game in which I felt I held the winning cards. The stake, roughly speaking, was the success of the voyage—for me; and he, I apprehended, had nothing to lose. Our intimacy matured rapidly, and before many words had been exchanged I perceived that the excellent Hermann had been making use of me. That simple and astute Teuton had been, it seems, holding me up to Falk in the light of a rival. I was young enough to be shocked at so much duplicity. " Did he tell you that in so many words? " I asked with indignation.

[93]

Hermann had not. He had given hints only; and of course it had not taken very much to alarm Falk; but, instead of declaring himself, he had taken steps to remove the family from under my influence. He was perfectly straightforward about it—as straightforward as a tile falling on your head. There was no duplicity in that man; and when I congratulated him on the perfection of his arrangements—even to the bribing of the wretched Johnson against me—he had a genuine movement of protest. Never bribed. He knew the man wouldn't work as long as he had a few cents in his pocket to get drunk on, and, naturally (he said— " *naturally* ") he let him have a dollar or two. He was himself a sailor, he said, and anticipated the view another sailor, like myself, was bound to take. On the other hand, he was sure that I should have to come to grief. He hadn't been knocking about for the last seven years up and down that river for nothing. It would have been no disgrace to me— but he asserted confidently I would have had my ship very awkwardly ashore at a spot two miles below the Great Pagoda. . . .

And with all that he had no ill-will. That was

evident. This was a crisis in which his only object had been to gain time—I fancy. And presently he mentioned that he had written for some jewellery, real good jewellery—had written to Hong-Kong for it. It would arrive in a day or two.

" Well, then," I said cheerily, " everything is all right. All you've got to do is to present it to the lady together with your heart, and live happy ever after."

Upon the whole he seemed to accept that view as far as the girl was concerned, but his eyelids drooped. There was still something in the way. For one thing Hermann disliked him so much. As to me, on the contrary, it seemed as though he could not praise me enough. Mrs. Hermann too. He didn't know why they disliked him so. It made everything most difficult.

I listened impassive, feeling more and more diplomatic. His speech was not transparently clear. He was one of those men who seem to live, feel, suffer in a sort of mental twilight. But as to being fascinated by the girl and possessed by the desire of home life with her—it was as clear as daylight. So much being at stake, he was afraid of putting it to the hazard of the declaration. Besides, there was something else. And with Hermann being so set against him . . .

" I see," I said thoughtfully, while my heart beat fast with the excitement of my diplomacy. " I don't mind sounding Hermann. In fact, to show you how mistaken you were, I am ready to do all I can for you in that way."

A light sigh escaped him. He drew his hands down his face, and it emerged, bony, unchanged of expression, as if all the tissues had been ossified. All the passion was in those big brown hands. He was satisfied. Then there was that other matter. If there were anybody on earth it was I who could persuade Hermann to take a reasonable view! I had a knowledge of the world and lots of experience. Hermann admitted this himself. And then I was a sailor too. Falk thought that a sailor would be able to understand certain things best. . . .

He talked as if the Hermanns had been living all their life in a rural hamlet, and I alone had been capable, with my practice in life, of a large and indulgent view of certain occurrences. That was what my diplomacy was leading me to. I began suddenly to dislike it.

"I say, Falk," I asked quite brusquely, "you haven't already a wife put away somewhere?"

The pain and disgust of his denial were very striking. Couldn't I understand that he was as respectable as any white man hereabouts; earning his living honestly. He was suffering from my suspicion, and the low undertone of his voice made his protestations sound very pathetic. For a moment he shamed me, but, my diplomacy notwithstanding, I seemed to develop a conscience, as if in very truth it were in my power to decide the success of this matrimonial enterprise. By pretending hard enough we come to believe anything—anything to our advantage. And I had been pretending very hard, because I meant yet to be towed safely down the river. But through conscience or stupidity, I couldn't help alluding to the Vanlo affair. "You acted rather badly there. Didn't you?" was what I ventured actually to say—for the logic of our conduct is always at the mercy of obscure and unforeseen impulses.

His dilated pupils swerved from my face, glancing at the window with a sort of scared fury. We heard behind the blinds the continuous and sudden clicking of ivory, a jovial murmur of many voices, and Schomberg's deep manly laugh.

" That confounded old woman of a hotel-keeper then would never, never let it rest!" Falk exclaimed. " Well, yes! It had happened two years ago." When it came to the point he owned he couldn't make up his mind to trust Fred Vanlo— no sailor, a bit of a fool too. He could not trust him, but, to stop his row, he had lent him enough money to pay all his debts before he left. I was greatly surprised to hear this. Then Falk could not be such a miser after all. So much the better for the girl. For a time he sat silent; then he picked up a card, and while looking at it he said:

" You need not think of anything bad. It was an accident. I've been unfortunate once."

" Then in heaven's name say nothing about it."

As soon as these words were out of my mouth I fancied I had said something immoral. He shook his head negatively. It had to be told. He considered it proper that the relations of the lady

should know. No doubt—I thought to myself—
had Miss Vanlo not been thirty and damaged by the
climate he would have found it possible to entrust
Fred Vanlo with this confidence. And then the figure of Hermann's niece appeared before my mind's
eye, with the wealth of her opulent form, her rich
youth, her lavish strength. With that powerful
and immaculate vitality, her girlish form must have
shouted aloud of life to that man, whereas poor
Miss Vanlo could only sing sentimental songs to
the strumming of a piano.

" And that Hermann hates me, I know it!" he
cried in his undertone, with a sudden recrudescence
of anxiety. " I must tell them. It is proper that
they should know. You would say so yourself."

He then murmured an utterly mysterious allusion to the necessity for peculiar domestic arrangements. Though my curiosity was excited I did not
want to hear any of his confidences. I feared he
might give me a piece of information that would
make my assumed *rôle* of match-maker odious—
however unreal it was. I was aware that he could
have the girl for the asking; and keeping down a
desire to laugh in his face, I expressed a confident

belief in my ability to argue away Hermann's dislike for him. " I am sure I can make it all right," I said. He looked very pleased.

And when we rose not a word had been said about towage! Not a word! The game was won and the honour was safe. Oh! blessed white cotton umbrella! We shook hands, and I was holding myself with difficulty from breaking into a step dance of joy when he came back, striding all the length of the verandah, and said doubtfully:

" I say, captain, I have your word? You—you —won't turn round? "

Heavens! The fright he gave me. Behind his tone of doubt there was something desperate and menacing. The infatuated ass. But I was equal to the situation.

" My dear Falk," I said, beginning to lie with a glibness and effrontery that amazed me even at the time—" confidence for confidence." (He had made no confidences.) " I will tell you that I am already engaged to an extremely charming girl at home, and so you understand. . . ."

He caught my hand and wrung it in a crushing grip.

[100]

" Pardon me. I feel it every day more difficult to live alone . . ."

" On rice and fish," I interrupted smartly, giggling with the sheer nervousness of a danger escaped.

He dropped my hand as if it had become suddenly red hot. A moment of profound silence ensued, as though something extraordinary had happened.

" I promise you to obtain Hermann's consent," I faltered out at last, and it seemed to me that he could not help seeing through that humbugging promise. " If there's anything else to get over I shall endeavour to stand by you," I conceded further, feeling somehow defeated and overborne; " but you must do your best yourself."

" I have been unfortunate once," he muttered unemotionally, and turning his back on me he went away, thumping slowly the plank floor as if his feet had been shod with iron.

Next morning, however, he was lively enough as man-boat, a combination of splashing and shouting; of the insolent commotion below with the steady overbearing glare of the silent head-piece

[101]

above. He turned us out most unnecessarily at an
ungodly hour, but it was nearly eleven in the morning before he brought me up a cable's length from
Hermann's ship. And he did it very badly too, in
a hurry, and nearly contriving to miss altogether
the patch of good holding ground, because, for-
sooth, he had caught sight of Hermann's niece on
the poop. And so did I; and probably as soon as
he had seen her himself. I saw the modest, sleek
glory of the tawny head, and the full, grey shape
of the girlish print frock she filled so perfectly, so
satisfactorily, with the seduction of unfaltering
curves—a very nymph of Diana the Huntress.
And *Diana* the ship sat, high-walled and as solid
as an institution, on the smooth level of the water,
the most uninspiring and respectable craft upon
the seas, useful and ugly, devoted to the support
of domestic virtues like any grocer's shop on shore.
At once Falk steamed away; for there was some
work for him to do. He would return in the evening.

He ranged close by us, passing out dead slow,
without a hail. The beat of the paddle-wheels re-
verberating amongst the stony islets, as if from the

ruined walls of a vast arena, filled the anchorage confusedly with the clapping sounds of a mighty and leisurely applause. Abreast of Hermann's ship he stopped the engines; and a profound silence reigned over the rocks, the shore and the sea, for the time it took him to raise his hat aloft before the nymph of the grey print frock. I had snatched up my binoculars, and I can answer for it she didn't stir a limb, standing by the rail shapely and erect, with one of her hands grasping a rope at the height of her head, while the way of the tug carried slowly past her the lingering and profound homage of the man. There was for me an enormous significance in the scene, the sense of having witnessed a solemn declaration. The die was cast. After such a manifestation he couldn't back out. And I reflected that it was nothing whatever to me now. With a rush of black smoke belching suddenly out of the funnel, and a mad swirl of paddle-wheels provoking a burst of weird and precipitated clapping, the tug shot out of the desolate arena. The rocky islets lay on the sea like the heaps of a cyclopean ruin on a plain; the centipedes and scorpions lurked under the stones; there was not a single blade of grass

[103]

in sight anywhere, not a single lizard sunning himself on a boulder by the shore. When I looked
again at Hermann's ship the girl had disappeared.
I could not detect the smallest dot of a bird on the
immense sky, and the flatness of the land continued
the flatness of the sea to the naked line of the horizon.

This is the setting now inseparably connected
with my knowledge of Falk's misfortune. My diplomacy had brought me there, and now I had only
to wait the time for taking up the *rôle* of an ambassador. My diplomacy was a success; my ship was
safe; old Gambril would probably live; a feeble
sound of a tapping hammer came intermittently
from the *Diana*. During the afternoon I looked
at times at the old homely ship, the faithful nurse
of Hermann's progeny, or yawned towards the distant temple of Buddha, like a lonely hillock on the
plain, where shaven priests cherish the thoughts of
that Annihilation which is the worthy reward of us
all. Unfortunate! He had been unfortunate once.
Well, that was not so bad as life goes. And what
the devil could be the nature of that misfortune?
I remembered that I had known a man before who

had declared himself to have fallen, years ago, a victim to misfortune; but this misfortune, whose effects appeared permanent (he looked desperately hard up) when considered dispassionately, seemed indistinguishable from a breach of trust. Could it be something of that nature? Apart, however, from the utter improbability that he would offer to talk of it even to his future uncle-in-law, I had a strange feeling that Falk's physique unfitted him for that sort of delinquency. As the person of Hermann's niece exhaled the profound physical charm of feminine form, so her adorer's big frame embodied to my senses the hard, straight masculinity that would conceivably kill but would not condescend to cheat. The thing was obvious. I might just as well have suspected the girl of a curvature of the spine. And I perceived that the sun was about to set.

The smoke of Falk's tug hove in sight, far away at the mouth of the river. It was time for me to assume the character of an ambassador, and the negotiation would not be difficult except in the matter of keeping my countenance. It was all too extravagantly nonsensical, and I conceived that it would be best to compose for myself a grave demeanour. I practised this in my boat as I went along, but the bashfulness that came secretly upon me the moment I stepped on the deck of the *Diana* is inexplicable. As soon as we had exchanged greetings Hermann asked me eagerly if I knew whether Falk had found his white parasol.

"He's going to bring it to you himself directly," I said with great solemnity. "Meantime I am charged with an important message for which he begs your favourable consideration. He is in love with your niece. . . ."

"*Ach So!*" he hissed with an animosity that made my assumed gravity change into the most genuine concern. What meant this tone? And I hurried on.

"He wishes, with your consent of course, to ask her to marry him at once—before you leave here, that is. He would speak to the Consul."

Hermann sat down and smoked violently. Five minutes passed in that furious meditation, and then, taking the long pipe out of his mouth, he burst into a hot diatribe against Falk—against his cupidity, his stupidity (a fellow that can hardly

be got to say " yes " or " no " to the simplest question)—against his outrageous treatment of the
shipping in port (because he saw they were at his
mercy)—and against his manner of walking,
which to his (Hermann's) mind showed a conceit
positively unbearable. The damage to the old
Diana was not forgotten, of course, and there was
nothing of any nature said or done by Falk (even
to the last offer of refreshment in the hotel) that
did not seem to have been a cause of offence.
" Had the cheek " to drag him (Hermann) into
that coffee-room; as though a drink from him could
make up for forty-seven dollars and fifty cents of
damage in the cost of wood alone—not counting
two days' work for the carpenter. Of course he
would not stand in the girl's way. He was going
home to Germany. There were plenty of poor
girls walking about in Germany.

" He's very much in love," was all I found to
say.

" Yes," he cried. " And it is time too after making himself and me talked about ashore the last
voyage I was here, and then now again; coming on

board every evening unsettling the girl's mind, and saying nothing. What sort of conduct is that?"

The seven thousand dollars the fellow was always talking about did not, in his opinion, justify such behaviour. Moreover, nobody had seen them. He (Hermann) seriously doubted if there were seven thousand cents, and the tug, no doubt, was mortgaged up to the top of the funnel to the firm of Siegers. But let that pass. He wouldn't stand in the girl's way. Her head was so turned that she had become no good to them of late. Quite unable even to put the children to bed without her aunt. It was bad for the children; they got unruly; and yesterday he actually had to give Gustav a thrashing.

For that, too, Falk was made responsible apparently. And looking at my Hermann's heavy, puffy, good-natured face, I knew he would not exert himself till greatly exasperated, and, therefore, would thrash very hard, and being fat would resent the necessity. How Falk had managed to turn the girl's head was more difficult to understand. I supposed Hermann would know. And then hadn't there been Miss Vanlo? It could not be his silvery

tongue, or the subtle seduction of his manner; he
had no more of what is called " manner " than an
animal—which, however, on the other hand, is
never, and can never be called vulgar. Therefore
it must have been his bodily appearance, exhibiting
a virility of nature as exaggerated as his beard, and
resembling a sort of constant ruthlessness. It was
seen in the very manner he lolled in the chair. He
meant no offence, but his intercourse was characterised by that sort of frank disregard of suscepti-
bilities a man of seven foot six, living in a world of
dwarfs, would naturally assume, without in the
least wishing to be unkind. But amongst men of
his own stature, or nearly, this frank use of his ad-
vantages, in such matters as the awful towage bills
for instance, caused much impotent gnashing of
teeth. When attentively considered it seemed appalling at times. He was a strange beast. But
maybe women liked it. Seen in that light he was
well worth taming, and I suppose every woman at
the bottom of her heart considers herself as a tamer
of strange beasts. But Hermann arose with pre-
cipitation to carry the news to his wife. I had
barely the time, as he made for the cabin door, to

grab him by the seat of his inexpressibles. I begged him to wait till Falk in person had spoken with him. There remained some small matter to talk over, as I understood.

He sat down again at once, full of suspicion.

"What matter?" he said surlily. "I have had enough of his nonsense. There's no matter at all, as he knows very well; the girl has nothing in the world. She came to us in one thin dress when my brother died, and I have a growing family."

"It can't be anything of that kind," I opined. "He's desperately enamoured of your niece. I don't know why he did not say so before. Upon my word, I believe it is because he was afraid to lose, perhaps, the felicity of sitting near her on your quarter deck."

I intimated my conviction that his love was so great as to be in a sense cowardly. The effects of a great passion are unaccountable. It has been known to make a man timid. But Hermann looked at me as if I had foolishly raved; and the twilight was dying out rapidly.

"You don't believe in passion, do you, Hermann?" I said cheerily. "The passion of fear will make a cornered rat courageous. Falk's in a corner. He will take her off your hands in one thin frock just as she came to you. And after ten years' service it isn't a bad bargain," I added.

Far from taking offence, he resumed his air of civic virtue. The sudden night came upon him while he stared placidly along the deck, bringing in contact with his thick lips, and taking away again after a jet of smoke, the curved mouthpiece fitted to the stem of his pipe. The night came upon him and buried in haste his whiskers, his globular eyes, his puffy pale face, his fat knees and the vast flat slippers on his fatherly feet. Only his short arms in respectable white shirt-sleeves remained very visible, propped up like the flippers of a seal reposing on the strand.

" Falk wouldn't settle anything about repairs. Told me to find out first how much wood I should require and he would see," he remarked; and after he had spat peacefully in the dusk we heard over the water the beat of the tug's floats. There is, on a calm night, nothing more suggestive of fierce and headlong haste than the rapid sound made by the paddle-wheels of a boat threshing her way through a quiet sea; and the approach of Falk towards his fate seemed to be urged by an impatient and passionate desire. The engines must have been driven to the very utmost of their revolutions. We heard them slow down at last, and, vaguely, the white hull of the tug appeared moving against the black islets, whilst a slow and rhythmical clapping as of thousands of hands rose on all sides. It ceased all at once, just before Falk brought her up. A single brusque splash was followed by the long drawn rumbling of iron links running through the hawse pipe. Then a solemn silence fell upon the Roadstead.

" He will soon be here," I murmured, and after that we waited for him without a word. Meantime, raising my eyes, I beheld the glitter of a lofty sky above the *Diana's* mastheads. The multitude of stars gathered into clusters, in rows, in lines, in masses, in groups, shone all together, unanimously —and the few isolated ones, blazing by themselves in the midst of dark patches, seemed to be of a superior kind and of an inextinguishable nature. But long striding footsteps were heard hastening along the deck; the high bulwarks of the *Diana* made a deeper darkness. We rose from our chairs quickly, and Falk, appearing before us, all in white, stood still.

Nobody spoke at first, as though we had been covered with confusion. His arrival was fiery, but his white bulk, of indefinite shape and without features, made him loom up like a man of snow.

" The captain here has been telling me . . ." Hermann began in a homely and amicable voice; and Falk had a low, nervous laugh. His cool, negligent undertone had no inflexions, but the strength of a powerful emotion made him ramble in his speech. He had always desired a home. It was difficult to live alone, though he was not answerable. He was domestic; there had been difficulties; but since he had seen Hermann's niece he found that it had become at last impossible to live by himself. " I mean—impossible," he repeated with no sort of emphasis and only with the slightest of pauses, but the word fell into my mind with the force of a new idea.

" I have not said anything to her yet," Hermann observed quietly. And Falk dismissed this by a " That's all right. Certainly. Very proper."

FALK

There was a necessity for perfect frankness—in marrying, especially. Hermann seemed attentive, but he seized the first opportunity to ask us into the cabin. " And by-the-by, Falk," he said innocently, as we passed in, " the timber came to no less than forty-seven dollars and fifty cents."

Falk, uncovering his head, lingered in the passage. " Some other time," he said; and Hermann nudged me angrily—I don't know why. The girl alone in the cabin sat sewing at some distance from the table. Falk stopped short in the doorway. Without a word, without a sign, without the slightest inclination of his bony head, by the silent intensity of his look alone, he seemed to lay his herculean frame at her feet. Her hands sank slowly on her lap, and raising her clear eyes, she let her soft, beaming glance enfold him from head to foot like a slow and pale caress. He was very hot when he sat down; she, with bowed head, went on with her sewing; her neck was very white under the light of the lamp; but Falk, hiding his face in the palms of his hands, shuddered faintly. He drew them down, even to his beard, and his uncovered eyes astonished me by their tense and irrational expres-

[114]

sion—as though he had just swallowed a heavy
gulp of alcohol. It passed away while he was
binding us to secrecy. Not that he cared, but he
did not like to be spoken about; and I looked at the
girl's marvellous, at her wonderful, at her regal
hair, plaited tight into that one astonishing and
maidenly tress. Whenever she moved her well-
shaped head it would stir stiffly to and fro on her
back. The thin cotton sleeve fitted the irreproach-
able roundness of her arm like a skin; and her very
dress, stretched on her bust, seemed to palpitate
like a living tissue with the strength of vitality ani-
mating her body. How good her complexion was,
the outline of her soft cheek and the small convo-
luted conch of her rosy ear! To pull her needle she
kept the little finger apart from the others; it
seemed a waste of power to see her sewing—eternally sewing—with that industrious and precise
movement of her arm, going on eternally upon all
the oceans, under all the skies, in innumerable har-
bours. And suddenly I heard Falk's voice declare
that he could not marry a woman unless she knew
of something in his life that had happened ten
years ago. It was an accident. An unfortunate ac-

[115]

cident. It would affect the domestic arrangements of their home, but, once told, it need not be alluded to again for the rest of their lives. "I should want my wife to feel for me," he said. "It has made me unhappy." And how could he keep the knowledge of it to himself—he asked us—perhaps through years and years of companionship? What sort of companionship would that be? He had thought it over. A wife must know. Then why not at once? He counted on Hermann's kindness for presenting the affair in the best possible light. And Hermann's countenance, mystified before, became very sour. He stole an inquisitive glance at me. I shook my head blankly. Some people thought, Falk went on, that such an experience changed a man for the rest of his life. He couldn't say. It was hard, awful, and not to be forgotten, but he did not think himself a worse man than before. Only he talked in his sleep now, he believed. . . . At last I began to think he had accidentally killed some one; perhaps a friend—his own father maybe; when he went on to say that probably we were aware he never touched meat. Throughout he spoke English, of course on my account.

He swayed forward heavily.

The girl, with her hands raised before her pale eyes, was threading her needle. He glanced at her, and his mighty trunk overshadowed the table, bringing nearer to us the breadth of his shoulders, the thickness of his neck, and that incongruous, anchorite head, burnt in the desert, hollowed and lean as if by excesses of vigils and fasting. His beard flowed imposingly downwards, out of sight, between the two brown hands gripping the edge of the table, and his persistent glance made sombre by the wide dilations of the pupils, fascinated.

" Imagine to yourselves," he said in his ordinary voice, " that I have eaten man."

I could only ejaculate a faint " Ah!" of complete enlightenment. But Hermann, dazed by the excessive shock, actually murmured, " Himmel! What for? "

" It was my terrible misfortune to do so," said Falk in a measured undertone. The girl, unconscious, sewed on. Mrs. Hermann was absent in one of the state-rooms, sitting up with Lena, who was feverish; but Hermann suddenly put both his hands up with a jerk. The embroidered calotte fell, and, in the twinkling of an eye, he had rumpled his hair all ends up in a most extravagant manner. In this state he strove to speak; with every effort his eyes seemed to start further out of their sockets; his head looked like a mop. He choked, gasped, swallowed, and managed to shriek out the one word, " Beast! "

From that moment till Falk went out of the cabin the girl, with her hands folded on the work lying in her lap, never took her eyes off him. His own, in the blindness of his heart, darted all over the cabin, only seeking to avoid the sight of Hermann's raving. It was ridiculous, and was made almost terrible by the stillness of every other person present. It was contemptible, and was made appalling by the man's overmastering horror of this awful sincerity, coming to him suddenly, with the confession of such a fact. He walked with great strides; he gasped. He wanted to know from Falk how dared he to come and tell him this? Did he think himself a proper person to be sitting in this cabin where his wife and children lived? Tell his niece! Expected him to tell his niece! His own brother's daughter! Shameless! Did I ever hear tell of such impudence?—he appealed to me. "This man here ought to have gone and hidden himself out of sight instead of . . ."

"But it's a great misfortune for me. But it's a great misfortune for me," Falk would ejaculate from time to time.

However, Hermann kept on running frequently against the corners of the table. At last he lost a slipper, and crossing his arms on his breast, walked up with one stocking foot very close to Falk, in order to ask him whether he did think there was anywhere on earth a woman abandoned enough to mate with such a monster. "Did he? Did he? Did he?" I tried to restrain him. He tore himself out of my hands; he found his slipper, and, endeavouring to put it on, stormed standing on one leg—and Falk, with a face unmoved and averted eyes, grasped all his mighty beard in one vast palm.

"Was it right then for me to die myself?" he asked thoughtfully. I laid my hand on his shoulder.

"Go away," I whispered imperiously, without any clear reason for this advice, except that I

wished to put an end to Hermann's odious noise.
" Go away."

He looked searchingly for a moment at Hermann
before he made a move. I left the cabin too to see
him out of the ship. But he hung about the quarter-deck.

" It is my misfortune," he said in a steady
voice.

" You were stupid to blurt it out in such a manner. After all, we don't hear such confidences
every day."

" What does the man mean? " he mused in deep
undertones. " Somebody had to die—but why
me? "

He remained still for a time in the dark—silent;
almost invisible. All at once he pinned my elbows
to my sides. I felt utterly powerless in his grip,
and his voice, whispering in my ear, vibrated.

" It's worse than hunger. Captain, do you know
what that means? And I could kill then—or be
killed. I wish the crowbar had smashed my skull
ten years ago. And I've got to live now. Without
her. Do you understand? Perhaps many years.
But how? What can be done? If I had allowed

myself to look at her once I would have carried her off before that man in my hands—like this."

I felt myself snatched off the deck, then suddenly dropped—and I staggered backwards, feeling bewildered and bruised. What a man! All was still; he was gone. I heard Hermann's voice declaiming in the cabin, and I went in.

I could not at first make out a single word, but Mrs. Hermann, who, attracted by the noise, had come in some time before, with an expression of surprise and mild disapproval depicted broadly on her face, was giving now all the signs of profound, helpless agitation. Her husband shot a string of guttural words at her, and instantly putting out one hand to the bulkhead as if to save herself from falling, she clutched the loose bosom of her dress with the other. He harangued the two women extraordinarily, with much of his shirt hanging out of his waistbelt, stamping his foot, turning from one to the other, sometimes throwing both his arms together, straight up above his rumpled hair, and keeping them in that position while he uttered a passage of loud denunciation; at others folding them tight across his breast—and then he hissed

with indignation, elevating his shoulders and pro-
truding his head. The girl was crying.

She had not changed her attitude. From her
steady eyes that, following Falk in his retreat, had
remained fixed wistfully on the cabin door, the
tears fell rapid, thick, on her hands, on the work in
her lap, warm and gentle like a shower in spring.
She wept without grimacing, without noise—very
touching, very quiet, with something more of pity
than of pain in her face, as one weeps in compassion
rather than in grief—and Hermann, before her,
declaimed. I caught several times the word
" Mensch," man ; and also " Fressen," which last I
looked up afterwards in my dictionary. It means
" Devour." Hermann seemed to be requesting an
answer of some sort from her ; his whole body
swayed. She remained mute and perfectly still ;
at last his agitation gained her ; she put the palms
of her hands together, her full lips parted, no
sound came. His voice scolded shrilly, his arms
went like a windmill—suddenly he shook a thick
fist at her. She burst out into loud sobs. He
seemed stupefied.

Mrs. Hermann rushed forward babbling rapidly. The two women fell on each other's necks, and, with an arm round her niece's waist, she led her away. Her own eyes were simply streaming, her face was flooded. She shook her head back at me negatively, I wonder why to this day. The girl's head dropped heavily on her shoulder. They disappeared.

Then Hermann sat down and stared at the cabin floor.

"We don't know all the circumstances," I ventured to break the silence. He retorted tartly that he didn't want to know of any. According to his ideas no circumstances could excuse a crime—and certainly not such a crime. This was the opinion generally received. The duty of a human being was to starve. Falk therefore was a beast, an animal; base, low, vile, despicable, shameless, and deceitful. He had been deceiving him since last year. He was, however, inclined to think that Falk must have gone mad quite recently; for no sane person, without necessity, uselessly, for no earthly reason, and regardless of another's self-respect and peace of mind, would own to having devoured human flesh. "Why tell?" he cried. "Who was asking him?" It showed Falk's brutality because after all he had selfishly caused him (Hermann) much pain. He would have preferred not to know that such an unclean creature had been in the habit of caressing his children. He hoped I would say nothing of all this ashore, though. He wouldn't like it to get about that he had been intimate with an eater of men—a common cannibal. As to the scene he had made (which I judged quite unnecessary) he was not going to inconvenience and restrain himself for a fellow that went about courting and upsetting girls' heads, while he knew all the time that no decent housewifely girl could think of marrying him. At least he (Hermann) could not conceive how any girl could. Fancy Lena! . . . No, it was impossible. The thoughts that would come into their heads every time they sat down to a meal. Horrible! Horrible!

"You are too squeamish, Hermann," I said.

He seemed to think it was eminently proper to be squeamish if the word meant disgust at Falk's conduct; and turning up his eyes sentimentally he drew my attention to the horrible fate of the victims —the victims of that Falk. I said that I knew nothing about them. He seemed surprised. Could not anybody imagine without knowing? He—for instance—felt he would like to avenge them. But what if—said I—there had not been any? They might have died as it were, naturally—of starvation. He shuddered. But to be eaten—after death! To be devoured! He gave another deep shudder, and asked suddenly, "Do you think it is true?"

His indignation and his personality together would have been enough to spoil the reality of the most authentic thing. When I looked at him I doubted the story—but the remembrance of Falk's words, looks, gestures, invested it not only with an air of reality but with the absolute truth of primitive passion.

"It is true just as much as you are able to make it; and exactly in the way you like to make it. For my part, when I hear you clamouring about it, I don't believe it is true at all."

And I left him pondering. The men in my boat lying at the foot of *Diana's* side ladder told me that the captain of the tug had gone away in his gig some time ago.

FALK

I let my fellows pull an easy stroke; because of the heavy dew the clear sparkle of the stars seemed to fall on me cold and wetting. There was a sense of lurking gruesome horror somewhere in my mind, and it was mingled with clear and grotesque images. Schomberg's gastronomic tittle-tattle was responsible for these; and I half hoped I should never see Falk again. But the first thing my anchor-watchman told me was that the captain of the tug was on board. He had sent his boat away and was now waiting for me in the cuddy.

He was lying full length on the stern settee, his face buried in the cushions. I had expected to see it discomposed, contorted, despairing. It was nothing of the kind; it was just as I had seen it twenty times, steady and glaring from the bridge of the tug. It was immovably set and hungry, dominated like the whole man by the singleness of one instinct.

He wanted to live. He had always wanted to live. So we all do—but in us the instinct serves a complex conception, and in him this instinct existed alone. There is in such simple development a gigantic force, and like the pathos of a child's naïve

[126]

and uncontrolled desire. He wanted that girl, and the utmost that can be said for him was that he wanted that particular girl alone. I think I saw then the obscure beginning, the seed germinating in the soil of an unconscious need, the first shoot of that tree bearing now for a mature mankind the flower and the fruit, the infinite gradation in shades and in flavour of our discriminating love. He was a child. He was as frank as a child too. He was hungry for the girl, terribly hungry, as he had been terribly hungry for food.

Don't be shocked if I declare that in my belief it was the same need, the same pain, the same torture. We are in his case allowed to contemplate the foundation of all the emotions—that one joy which is to live, and the one sadness at the root of the innumerable torments. It was made plain by the way he talked. He had never suffered so. It was gnawing, it was fire; it was there, like this! And after pointing below his breastbone, he made a hard wringing motion with his hands. And I assure you that, seen as I saw it with my bodily eyes, it was anything but laughable. And again, as he was presently to tell me (alluding to an early incident of the disastrous voyage when some damaged meat had been flung overboard), he said that a time soon came when his heart ached (that was the expression he used), and he was ready to tear his hair out at the thought of all that rotten beef thrown away.

I had heard all this; I witnessed his physical struggles, seeing the working of the rack and hearing the true voice of pain. I witnessed it all patiently, because the moment I came into the cuddy he had called upon me to stand by him—and this, it seems, I had diplomatically promised.

His agitation was impressive and alarming in the little cabin, like the floundering of a great whale driven into a shallow cove in a coast. He stood up; he flung himself down headlong; he tried to tear the cushion with his teeth; and again hugging it fiercely to his face he let himself fall on the couch. The whole ship seemed to feel the shock of his despair; and I contemplated with wonder the lofty forehead, the noble touch of time on the uncovered temples, the unchanged hungry character of the face—so strangely ascetic and so incapable of portraying emotion.

[128]

What should he do? He had lived by being near her. He had sat—in the evening—I knew?—all his life! She sewed. Her head was bent—so. Her head—like this—and her arms. Ah! Had I seen? Like this.

He dropped on a stool, bowed his powerful neck whose nape was red, and with his hands stitched the air, ludicrous, sublimely imbecile and comprehensible.

And now he couldn't have her? No! That was too much. After thinking too that . . . What had he done? What was my advice? Take her by force? No? Mustn't he? Who was there then to kill him? For the first time I saw one of his features move; a fighting teeth-baring curl of the lip. . . . "Not Hermann, perhaps." He lost himself in thought as though he had fallen out of the world.

I may note that the idea of suicide apparently did not enter his head for a single moment. It occurred to me to ask:

"Where was it that this shipwreck of yours took place?"

"Down south," he said vaguely with a start.

"You are not down south now," I said. "Violence won't do. They would take her away from you in no time. And what was the name of the ship?"

"*Borgmester Dahl*," he said. "It was no shipwreck."

He seemed to be waking up by degrees from that trance, and waking up calmed.

"Not a shipwreck? What was it?"

"Break down," he answered, looking more like himself every moment. By this only I learned that it was a steamer. I had till then supposed they had been starving in boats or on a raft—or perhaps on a barren rock.

"She did not sink then?" I asked in surprise. He nodded. "We sighted the southern ice," he pronounced dreamily.

"And you alone survived?"

He sat down. "Yes. It was a terrible misfortune for me. Everything went wrong. All the men went wrong. I survived."

Remembering the things one reads of it was difficult to realise the true meaning of his answers. I ought to have seen at once—but I did not; so diffi-

cult is it for our minds, remembering so much, in-
structed so much, informed of so much, to get in
touch with the real actuality at our elbow. And
with my head full of preconceived notions as to
how a case of " cannibalism and suffering at sea "
should be managed I said—" You were then so
lucky in the drawing of lots? "

" Drawing of lots? " he said. " What lots? Do
you think I would have allowed my life to go for
the drawing of lots? "

Not if he could help it, I perceived, no matter
what other life went.

" It was a great misfortune. Terrible. Awful,"
he said. " Many heads went wrong, but the best
men would live."

" The toughest, you mean," I said. He considered the word. Perhaps it was strange to him,
though his English was so good.

" Yes," he asserted at last. " The best. It was
everybody for himself at last and the ship open to
all."

Thus from question to question I got the whole
story. I fancy it was the only way I could that
night have stood by him. Outwardly at least he

was himself again; the first sign of it was the return of that incongruous trick he had of drawing both his hands down his face—and it had its meaning now, with that slight shudder of the frame and the passionate anguish of these hands uncovering a hungry immovable face, the wide pupils of the intent, silent, fascinating eyes.

It was an iron steamer of a most respectable origin. The burgomaster of Falk's native town had built her. She was the first steamer ever launched there. The burgomaster's daughter had christened her. Country people drove in carts from miles around to see her. He told me all this. He got the berth as what we should call a chief mate. He seemed to think it had been a feather in his cap; and, in his own corner of the world, this lover of life was of good parentage.

The burgomaster had advanced ideas in the ship-owning line. At that time not every one would have known enough to think of despatching a cargo steamer to the Pacific. But he loaded her with pitch-pine deals and sent her off to hunt for her luck. Wellington was to be the first port, I fancy. It doesn't matter, because in latitude 44°

south and somewhere halfway between Good Hope
and New Zealand the tail shaft broke and the propeller dropped off.

They were steaming then with a fresh gale on
the quarter and all their canvas set, to help the engines. But by itself the sail power was not enough
to keep way on her. When the propeller went the
ship broached-to at once, and the masts got
whipped overboard.

The disadvantage of being dismasted consisted
in this, that they had nothing to hoist flags on to
make themselves visible at a distance. In the
course of the first few days several ships failed to
sight them; and the gale was drifting them out of
the usual track. The voyage had been, from the
first, neither very successful nor very harmonious.
There had been quarrels on board. The captain
was a clever, melancholic man, who had no unusual
grip on his crew. The ship had been amply provisioned for the passage, but, somehow or other,
several barrels of meat were found spoiled on opening, and had been thrown overboard soon after
leaving home, as a sanitary measure. Afterwards
the crew of the *Borgmester Dahl* thought of that

[133]

rotten carrion with tears of regret, covetousness and despair.

She drove south. To begin with, there had been an appearance of organisation, but soon the bonds of discipline became relaxed. A sombre idleness succeeded. They looked with sullen eyes at the horizon. The gales increased: she lay in the trough, the seas made a clean breach over her. On one frightful night, when they expected their hulk to turn over with them every moment, a heavy sea broke on board, deluged the store-rooms and spoiled the best part of the remaining provisions. It seems the hatch had not been properly secured. This instance of neglect is characteristic of utter discouragement. Falk tried to inspire some energy into his captain, but failed. From that time he retired more into himself, always trying to do his utmost in the situation. It grew worse. Gale succeeded gale, with black mountains of water hurling themselves on the *Borgmester Dahl*. Some of the men never left their bunks; many became quarrelsome. The chief engineer, an old man, refused to speak at all to anybody. Others shut themselves up in their berths to cry. On calm days the inert steamer

rolled on a leaden sea under a murky sky, or
showed, in sunshine, the squalor of sea waifs, the
dried white salt, the rust, the jagged broken
places. Then the gales came again. They kept
body and soul together on short rations. Once, an
English ship, scudding in a storm, tried to stand
by them, heaving-to pluckily under their lee. The
seas swept her decks; the men in oilskins clinging
to her rigging looked at them, and they made desperate signs over their shattered bulwarks. Suddenly her main-topsail went, yard and all, in a terrific squall; she had to bear up under bare poles,
and disappeared.

Other ships had spoken them before, but at first
they had refused to be taken off, expecting the assistance of some steamer. There were very few
steamers in those latitudes then; and when they
desired to leave this dead and drifting carcase, no
ship came in sight. They had drifted south out of
men's knowledge. They failed to attract the attention of a lonely whaler, and very soon the edge of
the polar ice-cap rose from the sea and closed the
southern horizon like a wall. One morning they
were alarmed by finding themselves floating

amongst detached pieces of ice. But the fear of sinking passed away like their vigour, like their hopes; the shocks of the floes knocking against the ship's side could not rouse them from their apathy: and the *Borgmester Dahl* drifted out again unharmed into open water. They hardly noticed the change.

The funnel had gone overboard in one of the heavy rolls; two of their three boats had disappeared, washed away in bad weather, and the davits swung to and fro, unsecured, with chafed rope's ends waggling to the roll. Nothing was done on board, and Falk told me how he had often listened to the water washing about the dark engine-room where the engines, stilled for ever, were decaying slowly into a mass of rust, as the stilled heart decays within the lifeless body. At first, after the loss of the motive power, the tiller had been thoroughly secured by lashings. But in course of time these had rotted, chafed, rusted, parting one by one: and the rudder, freed, banged heavily to and fro night and day, sending dull shocks through the whole frame of the vessel. This was dangerous. Nobody cared enough to lift a little finger. He told me that even now sometimes waking up at night, he fancied he could hear the dull vibrating thuds. The pintles carried away, and it dropped off at last.

The final catastrophe came with the sending off of their one remaining boat. It was Falk who had managed to preserve her intact, and now it was agreed that some of the hands should sail away into the track of the shipping to procure assistance. She was provisioned with all the food they could spare for the six who were to go. They waited for a fine day. It was long in coming. At last one morning they lowered her into the water.

Directly, in that demoralised crowd, trouble broke out. Two men who had no business there had jumped into the boat under the pretence of unhooking the tackles, while some sort of squabble arose on the deck amongst these weak, tottering spectres of a ship's company. The captain, who had been for days living secluded and unapproachable in the chart-room, came to the rail. He ordered the two men to come up on board and menaced them with his revolver. They pretended to obey, but suddenly cutting the boat's painter, gave a shove against the ship's side and made ready to hoist the sail.

"Shoot, sir! Shoot them down!" cried Falk— "and I will jump overboard to regain the boat." But the captain, after taking aim with an irresolute arm, turned suddenly away.

A howl of rage arose. Falk dashed into his cabin for his own pistol. When he returned it was too late. Two more men had leaped into the water, but the fellows in the boat beat them off with the oars, hoisted the boat's lug and sailed away. They were never heard of again.

Consternation and despair possessed the remaining ship's company, till the apathy of utter hopelessness re-asserted its sway. That day a fireman committed suicide, running up on deck with his throat cut from ear to ear, to the horror of all hands. He was thrown overboard. The captain had locked himself in the chart-room, and Falk, knocking vainly for admittance, heard him reciting over and over again the names of his wife and children, not as if calling upon them or commending them to God, but in a mechanical voice like an exercise of memory. Next day the doors of the

[138]

chart-room were swinging open to the roll of the ship, and the captain had disappeared. He must during the night have jumped into the sea. Falk locked both the doors and kept the keys.

The organised life of the ship had come to an end. The solidarity of the men had gone. They became indifferent to each other. It was Falk who took in hand the distribution of such food as remained. They boiled their boots for soup to eke out the rations, which only made their hunger more intolerable. Sometimes whispers of hate were heard passing between the languid skeletons that drifted endlessly to and fro, north and south, east and west, upon that carcase of a ship.

And in this lies the grotesque horror of this sombre story. The last extremity of sailors, overtaking a small boat or a frail craft, seems easier to bear, because of the direct danger of the seas. The confined space, the close contact, the imminent menace of the waves, seem to draw men together, in spite of madness, suffering and despair. But there was a ship—safe, convenient, roomy: a ship with beds, bedding, knives, forks, comfortable cabins, glass and china, and a complete cook's galley, pervaded, ruled and possessed by the pitiless spectre of starvation. The lamp oil had been drunk, the wicks cut up for food, the candles eaten. At night she floated dark in all her recesses, and full of fears. One day Falk came upon a man gnawing a splinter of pine wood. Suddenly he threw the piece of wood away, tottered to the rail, and fell over. Falk, too late to prevent the act, saw him claw the ship's side desperately before he went down. Next day another man did the same thing, after uttering horrible imprecations. But this one somehow managed to get hold of the broken rudder chains and hung on there, silently. Falk set about trying to save him, and all the time the man, holding with both hands, looked at him anxiously with his sunken eyes. Then, just as Falk was ready to put his hand on him, the man let go his hold and sank like a stone. Falk reflected on these sights. His heart revolted against the horror of death, and he said to himself that he would struggle for every precious minute of his life.

One afternoon—as the survivors lay about on the after deck—the carpenter, a tall man with a black beard, spoke of the last sacrifice. There was nothing eatable left on board. Nobody said a word to this; but that company separated quickly, these listless feeble spectres slunk off one by one to hide in fear of each other. Falk and the carpenter remained on deck together. Falk liked the big carpenter. He had been the best man of the lot, helpful and ready as long as there was anything to do, the longest hopeful, and had preserved to the last some vigour and decision of mind.

They did not speak to each other. Henceforth no voices were to be heard conversing sadly on board that ship. After a time the carpenter tottered away forward; but later on, Falk going to drink at the fresh-water pump, had the inspiration to turn his head. The carpenter had stolen upon him from behind, and, summoning all his strength, was aiming with a crowbar a blow at the back of his skull.

Dodging just in time, Falk made his escape and ran into his cabin. While he was loading his revolver there, he heard the sound of heavy blows struck upon the bridge. The locks of the chart-room doors were slight, they flew open, and the carpenter, possessing himself of the captain's revolver, fired a shot of defiance.

Falk was about to go on deck and have it out at once, when he remarked that one of the ports of his cabin commanded the approaches to the fresh-water pump. Instead of going out he remained in and secured the door. "The best man shall survive," he said to himself—and the other, he reasoned, must at some time or other come there to drink. These starving men would drink often to cheat the pangs of their hunger. But the carpenter too must have noticed the position of the port. They were the two best men in the ship, and the game was with them. All the rest of the day Falk saw no one and heard no sound. At night he strained his eyes. It was dark—he heard a rustling noise once, but he was certain that no one could have come near the pump. It was to the left of his deck port, and he could not have failed to see a man, for the night was clear and starry. He saw nothing; towards morning another faint noise made him suspicious. Deliberately and quietly he unlocked his door. He had not slept, and had not

FALK

given way to the horror of the situation. He
wanted to live.

But during the night the carpenter, without at
all trying to approach the pump, had managed to
creep quietly along the starboard bulwark, and,
unseen, had crouched down right under Falk's deck
port. When daylight came he rose up suddenly,
looked in, and putting his arm through the round
brass framed opening, fired at Falk within a foot.
He missed—and Falk, instead of attempting to
seize the arm holding the weapon, opened his door
unexpectedly, and with the muzzle of his long revolver nearly touching the other's side, shot him
dead.

The best man had survived. Both of them had
at the beginning just strength enough to stand on
their feet, and both had displayed pitiless resolu-
tion, endurance, cunning and courage—all the
qualities of classic heroism. At once Falk threw
overboard the captain's revolver. He was a born
monopolist. Then after the report of the two
shots, followed by a profound silence, there crept
out into the cold, cruel dawn of Antarctic regions,

FALK

from various hiding-places, over the deck of that
dismantled corpse of a ship floating on a grey sea
ruled by iron necessity and with a heart of ice—
there crept into view one by one, cautious, slow, ea-
ger, glaring, and unclean, a band of hungry and
livid skeletons. Falk faced them, the possessor of
the only fire-arm on board, and the second best man
—the carpenter—was lying dead between him and
them.

"He was eaten, of course," I said.

He bent his head slowly, shuddered a little, drawing his hands over his face, and said, "I had never
any quarrel with that man. But there were our
lives between him and me."

Why continue the story of that ship, that story
before which, with its fresh-water pump like a
spring of death, its man with the weapon, the sea
ruled by iron necessity, its spectral band swayed by
terror and hope, its mute and unhearing heaven?—
the fable of the *Flying Dutchman* with its conven-
tion of crime and its sentimental retribution fades
like a graceful wreath, like a wisp of white mist.
What is there to say that every one of us cannot
guess for himself? I believe Falk began by going

through the ship, revolver in hand, to annex all the matches. Those starving wretches had plenty of matches! He had no mind to have the ship set on fire under his feet, either from hate or from despair. He lived in the open, camping on the bridge, commanding all the after deck and the only approach to the pump. He lived! Some of the others lived too—concealed, anxious, coming out one by one from their hiding-places at the seductive sound of a shot. And he was not selfish. They shared, but only three of them all were alive when a whaler, returning from her cruising ground, nearly ran over the water-logged hull of the *Borgmester Dahl*, which, it seems, in the end had in some way sprung a leak in both her holds, but being loaded with deals could not sink.

"They all died," Falk said. "These three too, afterwards. But I would not die. All died, all! under this terrible misfortune. But was I too to throw away my life? Could I? Tell me, captain? I was alone there, quite alone, just like the others. Each man was alone. Was I to give up my revolver? Who to? Or was I to throw it into the sea? What would have been the good? Only the best man would survive. It was a great, terrible, and cruel misfortune."

He had survived! I saw him before me as though preserved for a witness to the mighty truth of an unerring and eternal principle. Great beads of perspiration stood on his forehead. And suddenly it struck the table with a heavy blow, as he fell forward throwing his hands out.

"And this is worse," he cried. "This is a worse pain! This is more terrible."

He made my heart thump with the profound conviction of his cries. And after he had left me alone I called up before my mental eye the image of the girl weeping silently, abundantly, patiently, and as if irresistibly. I thought of her tawny hair. I thought how, if unplaited, it would have covered her all round as low as the hips, like the hair of a siren. And she had bewitched him. Fancy a man who would guard his own life with the inflexibility of a pitiless and immovable fate, being brought to lament that once a crowbar had missed his skull! The sirens sing and lure to death, but this one had been weeping silently as if for the pity of his life. She was the tender and voiceless siren

of this appalling navigator. He evidently wanted
to live his whole conception of life. Nothing else
would do. And she too was a servant of that life
that, in the midst of death, cries aloud to our senses.
She was eminently fitted to interpret for him its
feminine side. And in her own way, and with her
own profusion of sensuous charms, she also seemed
to illustrate the eternal truth of an unerring principle. I don't know though what sort of principle
Hermann illustrated when he turned up early on
board my ship with a most perplexed air. It
struck me, however, that he too would do his best
to survive. He seemed greatly calmed on the subject of Falk, but still very full of it.

"What is it you said I was last night? You
know," he asked after some preliminary talk.
"Too—too—I don't know. A very funny word."

"Squeamish?" I suggested.

"Yes. What does it mean?"

"That you exaggerate things—to yourself.
Without inquiry, and so on."

He seemed to turn it over in his mind. We went
on talking. This Falk was the plague of his life.
Upsetting everybody like this! Mrs. Hermann

was unwell rather this morning. His niece was crying still. There was nobody to look after the children. He struck his umbrella on the deck. She would be like that for months. Fancy carrying all the way home, second class, a perfectly useless girl who is crying all the time. It was bad for Lena too, he observed; but on what grounds I could not guess. Perhaps of the bad example. That child was already sorrowing and crying enough over the rag doll. Nicholas was really the least sentimental person of the family.

" Why does she weep? " I asked.

" From pity," cried Hermann.

It was impossible to make out women. Mrs. Hermann was the only one he pretended to understand. She was very, very upset and doubtful.

" Doubtful about what? " I asked.

He averted his eyes and did not answer this. It was impossible to make them out. For instance, his niece was weeping for Falk. Now he (Hermann) would like to wring his neck—but then . . . He supposed he had too tender a heart. " Frankly," he asked at last, " what do you think of what we heard last night, captain? "

" In all these tales," I observed, " there is always a good deal of exaggeration."

And not letting him recover from his surprise I assured him that I knew all the details. He begged me not to repeat them. His heart was too tender. They made him feel unwell. Then, looking at his feet and speaking very slowly, he supposed that he need not see much of them after they were married. For, indeed, he could not bear the sight of Falk. On the other hand it was ridiculous to take home a girl with her head turned. A girl that weeps all the time and is of no help to her aunt.

" Now you will be able to do with one cabin only on your passage home," I said.

" Yes, I had thought of that," he said brightly, almost. " Yes! Himself, his wife, four children —one cabin might do. Whereas if his niece went . . ."

" And what does Mrs. Hermann say to it? " I inquired.

Mrs. Hermann did not know whether a man of that sort could make a girl happy—she had been greatly deceived in Captain Falk. She had been very upset last night.

Those good people did not seem to be able to retain an impression for a whole twelve hours. I assured him on my own personal knowledge that Falk possessed in himself all the qualities to make his niece's future prosperous. He said he was glad to hear this, and that he would tell his wife. Then the object of the visit came out. He wished me to help him to resume relations with Falk. His niece, he said, had expressed the hope I would do so in my kindness. He was evidently anxious that I should, for though he seemed to have forgotten nine-tenths of his last night's opinions and the whole of his indignation, yet he evidently feared to be sent to the right-about. "You told me he was very much in love," he concluded slyly, and leered in a sort of bucolic way.

"As soon as he had left my ship I called Falk on board by signal—the tug still lying at the anchorage. He took the news with calm gravity, as though he had all along expected the stars to fight for him in their courses.

I saw them once more together, and only once—on the quarter-deck of the *Diana*. Hermann sat smoking with a shirt-sleeved elbow hooked over the back of his chair. Mrs. Hermann was sewing alone. As Falk stepped over the gangway, Hermann's niece, with a slight swish of the skirt and a swift friendly nod to me, glided past my chair.

They met in sunshine abreast of the mainmast. He held her hands and looked down at them, and she looked up at him with her candid and unseeing glance. It seemed to me they had come together as if attracted, drawn and guided to each other by a mysterious influence. They were a complete couple. In her grey frock, palpitating with life, generous of form, olympian and simple, she was indeed the siren to fascinate that dark navigator, this ruthless lover of the five senses. From afar I seemed to feel the masculine strength with which he grasped those hands she had extended to him with a womanly swiftness. Lena, a little pale, nursing her beloved lump of dirty rags, ran towards her big friend; and then in the drowsy silence of the good old ship Mrs. Hermann's voice rang out so changed that it made me spin round in my chair to see what was the matter.

"Lena, come here!" she screamed. And this good-natured matron gave me a wavering glance, dark and full of fearsome distrust. The child ran back, surprised, to her knee. But the two, standing before each other in sunlight with clasped hands, had heard nothing, had seen nothing and no one. Three feet away from them in the shade a seaman sat on a spar, very busy splicing a strop, and dipping his fingers into a tar-pot, as if utterly unaware of their existence.

When I returned in command of another ship, some five years afterwards, Mr. and Mrs. Falk had left the place. I should not wonder if Schomberg's tongue had succeeded at last in scaring Falk away for good; and, indubitably, there was a tale still going about the town of a certain Falk, owner of a tug, who had won his wife at cards from the captain of an English ship.

AMY FOSTER

AMY FOSTER

AMY FOSTER

Kennedy is a country doctor, and lives in Colebrook, on the shores of Eastbay. The high
ground rising abruptly behind the red roofs of the
little town crowds the quaint High Street against
the wall which defends it from the sea. Beyond
the sea-wall there curves for miles in a vast and
regular sweep the barren beach of shingle, with the
village of Brenzett standing out darkly across the
water, a spire in a clump of trees; and still further
out the perpendicular column of a lighthouse, looking in the distance no bigger than a lead pencil,
marks the vanishing-point of the land. The country at the back of Brenzett is low and flat, but the
bay is fairly well sheltered from the seas, and occasionally a big ship, windbound or through stress
of weather, makes use of the anchoring ground a
mile and a half due north from you as you stand
at the back door of the " Ship Inn " in Brenzett.

A dilapidated windmill near by lifting its shattered arms from a mound no loftier than a rubbish heap, and a Martello tower squatting at the water's edge half a mile to the south of the Coastguard cottages, are familiar to the skippers of small craft. These are the official seamarks for the patch of trustworthy bottom represented on the Admiralty charts by an irregular oval of dots enclosing several figures six, with a tiny anchor engraved among them, and the legend " mud and shells " over all.

The brow of the upland overtops the square tower of the Colebrook Church. The slope is green and looped by a white road. Ascending along this road, you open a valley broad and shallow, a wide green trough of pastures and hedges merging inland into a vista of purple tints and flowing lines closing the view.

In this valley down to Brenzett and Colebrook and up to Darnford, the market town fourteen miles away, lies the practice of my friend Kennedy. He had begun life as surgeon in the Navy, and afterwards had been the companion of a famous traveller, in the days when there were continents with unexplored interiors. His papers on the

fauna and flora made him known to scientific socie-
ties. And now he had come to a country practice
—from choice. The penetrating power of his
mind, acting like a corrosive fluid, had destroyed
his ambition, I fancy. His intelligence is of a
scientific order, of an investigating habit, and of
that unappeasable curiosity which believes that
there is a particle of a general truth in every mystery.

A good many years ago now, on my return from
abroad, he invited me to stay with him. I came
readily enough, and as he could not neglect his
patients to keep me company, he took me on his
rounds—thirty miles or so of an afternoon, sometimes. I waited for him on the roads; the horse
reached after the leafy twigs, and, sitting high in
the dogcart, I could hear Kennedy's laugh through
the half-open door left open of some cottage. He
had a big, hearty laugh that would have fitted a
man twice his size, a brisk manner, a bronzed face,
and a pair of grey, profoundly attentive eyes. He
had the talent of making people talk to him freely,
and an inexhaustible patience in listening to their
tales.

One day, as we trotted out of a large village into a shady bit of road, I saw on our left hand a low, black cottage, with diamond panes in the windows, a creeper on the end wall, a roof of shingle, and some roses climbing on the rickety trellis-work of the tiny porch. Kennedy pulled up to a walk. A woman, in full sunlight, was throwing a dripping blanket over a line stretched between two old apple-trees. And as the bobtailed, long-necked chestnut, trying to get his head, jerked the left hand, covered by a thick dogskin glove, the doctor raised his voice over the hedge: "How's your child, Amy?"

I had the time to see her dull face, red, not with a mantling blush, but as if her flat cheeks had been vigorously slapped, and to take in the squat figure, the scanty, dusty brown hair drawn into a tight knot at the back of the head. She looked quite young. With a distinct catch in her breath, her voice sounded low and timid.

"He's well, thank you."

We trotted again. "A young patient of yours," I said; and the doctor, flicking the chestnut absently, muttered, "Her husband used to be."

"She seems a dull creature," I remarked list-lessly.

"Precisely," said Kennedy. "She is very pas-sive. It's enough to look at the red hands hanging at the end of those short arms, at those slow, prom-inent brown eyes, to know the inertness of her mind —an inertness that one would think made it ever-lastingly safe from all the surprises of imagina-tion. And yet which of us is safe? At any rate, such as you see her, she had enough imagination to fall in love. She's the daughter of one Isaac Foster, who from a small farmer has sunk into a shepherd; the beginning of his misfortunes dating from his runaway marriage with the cook of his widowed father—a well-to-do, apoplectic grazier, who passionately struck his name off his will, and had been heard to utter threats against his life. But this old affair, scandalous enough to serve as a motive for a Greek tragedy, arose from the simi-larity of their characters. There are other trage-dies, less scandalous and of a subtler poignancy, arising from irreconcilable differences and from that fear of the Incomprehensible that hangs over all our heads—over all our heads. . . ."

AMY FOSTER

The tired chestnut dropped into a walk; and the
rim of the sun, all red in a speckless sky, touched
familiarly the smooth top of a ploughed rise near
the road as I had seen it times innumerable touch
the distant horizon of the sea. The uniform
brownness of the harrowed field glowed with a rosy
tinge, as though the powdered clods had sweated
out in minute pearls of blood the toil of uncounted
ploughmen. From the edge of a copse a waggon
with two horses was rolling gently along the ridge.
Raised above our heads upon the sky-line, it loomed
up against the red sun, triumphantly big, enormous, like a chariot of giants drawn by two slow-
stepping steeds of legendary proportions. And
the clumsy figure of the man plodding at the head
of the leading horse projected itself on the background of the Infinite with a heroic uncouthness.
The end of his carter's whip quivered high up in
the blue. Kennedy discoursed.

" She's the eldest of a large family. At the age
of fifteen they put her out to service at the New
Barns Farm. I attended Mrs. Smith, the tenant's
wife, and saw that girl there for the first time.
Mrs. Smith, a genteel person with a sharp nose,

[160]

made her put on a black dress every afternoon. I don't know what induced me to notice her at all. There are faces that call your attention by a curious want of definiteness in their whole aspect, as, walking in a mist, you peer attentively at a vague shape which, after all, may be nothing more curious or strange than a signpost. The only peculiarity I perceived in her was a slight hesitation in her utterance, a sort of preliminary stammer which passes away with the first word. When sharply spoken to, she was apt to lose her head at once; but her heart was of the kindest. She had never been heard to express a dislike for a single human being, and she was tender to every living creature. She was devoted to Mrs. Smith, to Mr. Smith, to their dogs, cats, canaries; and as to Mrs. Smith's grey parrot, its peculiarities exercised upon her a positive fascination. Nevertheless, when that outlandish bird, attacked by the cat, shrieked for help in human accents, she ran out into the yard stopping her ears, and did not prevent the crime. For Mrs. Smith this was another evidence of her stupidity; on the other hand, her want of charm, in view of Smith's well-known frivolousness, was a great rec-

ommendation. Her short-sighted eyes would swim
with pity for a poor mouse in a trap, and she had
been seen once by some boys on her knees in the wet
grass helping a toad in difficulties. If it's true, as
some German fellow has said, that without phos-
phorus there is no thought, it is still more true that
there is no kindness of heart without a certain
amount of imagination. She had some. She had
even more than is necessary to understand suffering and to be moved by pity. She fell in love under circumstances that leave no room for doubt in
the matter; for you need imagination to form a
notion of beauty at all, and still more to discover
your ideal in an unfamiliar shape.

" How this aptitude came to her, what it did
feed upon, is an inscrutable mystery. She was
born in the village, and had never been further
away from it than Colebrook or perhaps Darnford.
She lived for four years with the Smiths. New
Barns is an isolated farmhouse a mile away from
the road, and she was content to look day after
day at the same fields, hollows, rises; at the trees
and the hedgerows; at the faces of the four men
about the farm, always the same—day after day,

month after month, year after year. She never showed a desire for conversation, and, as it seemed to me, she did not know how to smile. Sometimes of a fine Sunday afternoon she would put on her best dress, a pair of stout boots, a large grey hat trimmed with a black feather (I've seen her in that finery), seize an absurdly slender parasol, climb over two stiles, tramp over three fields and along two hundred yards of road—never further. There stood Foster's cottage. She would help her mother to give their tea to the younger children, wash up the crockery, kiss the little ones, and go back to the farm. That was all. All the rest, all the change, all the relaxation. She never seemed to wish for anything more. And then she fell in love. She fell in love silently, obstinately—perhaps helplessly. It came slowly, but when it came it worked like a powerful spell; it was love as the Ancients understood it: an irresistible and fateful impulse— a possession! Yes, it was in her to become haunted and possessed by a face, by a presence, fatally, as though she had been a pagan worshipper of form under a joyous sky—and to be awakened at last from that mysterious forgetfulness of self, from that enchantment, from that transport, by a fear resembling the unaccountable terror of a brute. . . ."

With the sun hanging low on its western limit, the expanse of the grass-lands framed in the counter-scarps of the rising ground took on a gorgeous and sombre aspect. A sense of penetrating sadness, like that inspired by a grave strain of music, disengaged itself from the silence of the fields. The men we met walked past slow, unsmiling, with downcast eyes, as if the melancholy of an over-burdened earth had weighted their feet, bowed their shoulders, borne down their glances.

" Yes," said the doctor to my remark, " one would think the earth is under a curse, since of all her children these that cling to her the closest are uncouth in body and as leaden of gait as if their very hearts were loaded with chains. But here on this same road you might have seen amongst these heavy men a being lithe, supple, and long-limbed, straight like a pine with something striving upwards in his appearance as though the heart within him had been buoyant. Perhaps it was only the force of the contrast, but when he was passing one of these villagers here, the soles of his feet did not seem to me to touch the dust of the road. He vaulted over the stiles, paced these slopes with a long elastic stride that made him noticeable at a great distance, and had lustrous black eyes. He was so different from the mankind around that, with his freedom of movement, his soft—a little startled, glance, his olive complexion and graceful bearing, his humanity suggested to me the nature of a woodland creature. He came from there."

The doctor pointed with his whip, and from the summit of the descent seen over the rolling tops of the trees in a park by the side of the road, appeared the level sea far below us, like the floor of an immense edifice inlaid with bands of dark ripple, with still trails of glitter, ending in a belt of glassy water at the foot of the sky. The light blur of smoke, from an invisible steamer, faded on the great clearness of the horizon like the mist of a breath on a mirror; and, inshore, the white sails of a coaster, with the appearance of disentangling themselves slowly from under the branches, floated clear of the foliage of the trees.

" Shipwrecked in the bay? " I said.

"Yes; he was a castaway. A poor emigrant from Central Europe bound to America and washed ashore here in a storm. And for him, who knew nothing of the earth, England was an undiscovered country. It was some time before he learned its name; and for all I know he might have expected to find wild beasts or wild men here, when, crawling in the dark over the sea-wall, he rolled down the other side into a dyke, where it was another miracle he didn't get drowned. But he struggled instinctively like an animal under a net, and this blind struggle threw him out into a field. He must have been, indeed, of a tougher fibre than he looked to withstand without expiring such buffetings, the violence of his exertions, and so much fear. Later on, in his broken English that resembled curiously the speech of a young child, he told me himself that he put his trust in God, believing he was no longer in this world. And truly—he would add—how was he to know? He fought his way against the rain and the gale on all fours, and crawled at last among some sheep huddled close under the lee of a hedge. They ran off in all directions, bleating in the darkness, and he welcomed the first familiar sound he heard on these shores. It must have been two in the morning then. And this is all we know of the manner of his landing, though he did not arrive unattended by any means. Only his grisly company did not begin to come ashore till much later in the day. . . ."

The doctor gathered the reins, clicked his tongue; we trotted down the hill. Then turning, almost directly, a sharp corner into the High Street, we rattled over the stones and were home.

Late in the evening Kennedy, breaking a spell of moodiness that had come over him, returned to the story. Smoking his pipe, he paced the long room from end to end. A reading-lamp concentrated all its light upon the papers on his desk; and, sitting by the open window, I saw, after the windless, scorching day, the frigid splendour of a hazy sea lying motionless under the moon. Not a whisper, not a splash, not a stir of the shingle, not a footstep, not a sigh came up from the earth below—never a sign of life but the scent of climbing jasmine; and Kennedy's voice, speaking behind me, passed through the wide casement, to vanish outside in a chill and sumptuous stillness.

". . . The relations of shipwrecks in the olden time tell us of much suffering. Often the castaways were only saved from drowning to die miserably from starvation on a barren coast; others suffered violent death or else slavery, passing through years of precarious existence with people to whom their strangeness was an object of suspicion, dislike or fear. We read about these things, and they are very pitiful. It is indeed hard upon a man to find himself a lost stranger, helpless, incomprehensible, and of a mysterious origin, in some obscure corner of the earth. Yet amongst all the adventurers shipwrecked in all the wild parts of the world there is not one, it seems to me, that ever had to suffer a fate so simply tragic as the man I am speaking of, the most innocent of adventurers cast out by the sea in the bight of this bay, almost within sight from this very window.

" He did not know the name of his ship. Indeed, in the course of time we discovered he did not even know that ships had names—' like Christian people '; and when, one day, from the top of the Talfourd Hill, he beheld the sea lying open to his view, his eyes roamed afar, lost in an air of wild surprise,

as though he had never seen such a sight before.
And probably he had not. As far as I could make
out, he had been hustled together with many others
on board an emigrant-ship lying at the mouth of
the Elbe, too bewildered to take note of his surroundings, too weary to see anything, too anxious
to care. They were driven below into the 'tween-
deck and battened down from the very start. It
was a low timber dwelling—he would say—with
wooden beams overhead, like the houses in his country, but you went into it down a ladder. It was
very large, very cold, damp and sombre, with places
in the manner of wooden boxes where people had to
sleep, one above another, and it kept on rocking all
ways at once all the time. He crept into one of
these boxes and laid down there in the clothes in
which he had left his home many days before, keeping his bundle and his stick by his side. People
groaned, children cried, water dripped, the lights
went out, the walls of the place creaked, and everything was being shaken so that in one's little box
one dared not lift one's head. He had lost touch
with his only companion (a young man from the
same valley, he said), and all the time a great noise

of wind went on outside and heavy blows fell—
boom! boom! An awful sickness overcame him,
even to the point of making him neglect his prayers. Besides, one could not tell whether it was
morning or evening. It seemed always to be night
in that place.

" Before that he had been travelling a long, long
time on the iron track. He looked out of the window, which had a wonderfully clear glass in it, and
the trees, the houses, the fields, and the long roads
seemed to fly round and round about him till his
head swam. He gave me to understand that he had
on his passage beheld uncounted multitudes of people—whole nations—all dressed in such clothes as
the rich wear. Once he was made to get out of the
carriage, and slept through a night on a bench in
a house of bricks with his bundle under his head;
and once for many hours he had to sit on a floor of
flat stones dozing, with his knees up and with his
bundle between his feet. There was a roof over him,
which seemed made of glass, and was so high that
the tallest mountain-pine he had ever seen would
have had room to grow under it. Steam-machines
rolled in at one end and out at the other. People

swarmed more than you can see on a feast-day
round the miraculous Holy Image in the yard of
the Carmelite Convent down in the plains where,
before he left his home, he drove his mother in a
wooden cart—a pious old woman who wanted to
offer prayers and make a vow for his safety. He
could not give me an idea of how large and lofty
and full of noise and smoke and gloom, and clang
of iron, the place was, but some one had told him
it was called Berlin. Then they rang a bell, and
another steam-machine came in, and again he was
taken on and on through a land that wearied his
eyes by its flatness without a single bit of a hill to
be seen anywhere. One more night he spent shut
up in a building like a good stable with a litter of
straw on the floor, guarding his bundle amongst a
lot of men, of whom not one could understand a
single word he said. In the morning they were all
led down to the stony shores of an extremely broad
muddy river, flowing not between hills but between
houses that seemed immense. There was a steam-
machine that went on the water, and they all stood
upon it packed tight, only now there were with
them many women and children who made much

noise. A cold rain fell, the wind blew in his face; he was wet through, and his teeth chattered. He and the young man from the same valley took each other by the hand.

" They thought they were being taken to America straight away, but suddenly the steam-machine bumped against the side of a thing like a house on the water. The walls were smooth and black, and there uprose, growing from the roof as it were, bare trees in the shape of crosses, extremely high. That's how it appeared to him then, for he had never seen a ship before. This was the ship that was going to swim all the way to America. Voices shouted, everything swayed; there was a ladder dipping up and down. He went up on his hands and knees in mortal fear of falling into the water below, which made a great splashing. He got separated from his companion, and when he descended into the bottom of that ship his heart seemed to melt suddenly within him.

" It was then also, as he told me, that he lost contact for good and all with one of those three men who the summer before had been going about through all the little towns in the foothills of his

[172]

country. They would arrive on market days driving in a peasant's cart, and would set up an office in an inn or some other Jew's house. There were three of them, of whom one with a long beard looked venerable; and they had red cloth collars round their necks and gold lace on their sleeves like Government officials. They sat proudly behind a long table; and in the next room, so that the common people shouldn't hear, they kept a cunning telegraph machine, through which they could talk to the Emperor of America. The fathers hung about the door, but the young men of the mountains would crowd up to the table asking many questions, for there was work to be got all the year round at three dollars a day in America, and no military service to do.

"But the American Kaiser would not take everybody. Oh, no! He himself had a great difficulty in getting accepted, and the venerable man in uniform had to go out of the room several times to work the telegraph on his behalf. The American Kaiser engaged him at last at three dollars, he being young and strong. However, many able young men backed out, afraid of the great distance; besides, those only who had some money could be taken. There were some who sold their huts and their land because it cost a lot of money to get to America; but then, once there, you had three dollars a day, and if you were clever you could find places where true gold could be picked up on the ground. His father's house was getting over full. Two of his brothers were married and had children. He promised to send money home from America by post twice a year. His father sold an old cow, a pair of piebald mountain ponies of his own raising, and a cleared plot of fair pasture land on the sunny slope of a pine-clad pass to a Jew inn-keeper in order to pay the people of the ship that took men to America to get rich in a short time.

"He must have been a real adventurer at heart, for how many of the greatest enterprises in the conquest of the earth had for their beginning just such a bargaining away of the paternal cow for the mirage or true gold far away! I have been telling you more or less in my own words what I learned fragmentarily in the course of two or three years, during which I seldom missed an opportunity of a

[174]

friendly chat with him. He told me this story of his adventure with many flashes of white teeth and lively glances of black eyes, at first in a sort of anxious baby-talk, then, as he acquired the language, with great fluency, but always with that singing, soft, and at the same time vibrating intonation that instilled a strangely penetrating power into the sound of the most familiar English words, as if they had been the words of an unearthly language. And he always would come to an end, with many emphatic shakes of his head, upon that awful sensation of his heart melting within him directly he set foot on board that ship. Afterwards there semed to come for him a period of blank ignorance, at any rate as to facts. No doubt he must have been abominably sea-sick and abominably unhappy —this soft and passionate adventurer, taken thus out of his knowledge, and feeling bitterly as he lay in his emigrant bunk his utter loneliness; for his was a highly sensitive nature. The next thing we know of him for certain is that he had been hiding in Hammond's pig-pound by the side of the road to Norton six miles, as the crow flies, from the sea. Of these experiences he was unwilling to speak:

they seemed to have seared into his soul a sombre sort of wonder and indignation. Through the rumours of the country-side, which lasted for a good many days after his arrival, we know that the fishermen of West Colebrook had been disturbed and startled by heavy knocks against the walls of weatherboard cottages, and by a voice crying piercingly strange words in the night. Several of them turned out even, but, no doubt, he had fled in sudden alarm at their rough angry tones hailing each other in the darkness. A sort of frenzy must have helped him up the steep Norton hill. It was he, no doubt, who early the following morning had been seen lying (in a swoon, I should say) on the roadside grass by the Brenzett carrier, who actually got down to have a nearer look, but drew back, intimidated by the perfect immobility, and by something queer in the aspect of that tramp, sleeping so still under the showers. As the day advanced, some children came dashing into school at Norton in such a fright that the schoolmistress went out and spoke indignantly to a ' horrid-looking man ' on the road. He edged away, hanging his head, for a few steps, and then suddenly ran off with ex-

[176]

traordinary fleetness. The driver of Mr. Brad-
ley's milk-cart made no secret of it that he had
lashed with his whip at a hairy sort of gipsy fellow who, jumping up at a turn of the road by the
Vents, made a snatch at the pony's bridle. And
he caught him a good one too, right over the face,
he said, that made him drop down in the mud a
jolly sight quicker than he had jumped up; but it
was a good half-a-mile before he could stop the
pony. Maybe that in his desperate endeavours to
get help, and in his need to get in touch with some
one, the poor devil had tried to stop the cart. Also
three boys confessed afterwards to throwing stones
at a funny tramp, knocking about all wet and
muddy, and, it seemed, very drunk, in the narrow
deep lane by the limekilns. All this was the talk of
three villages for days; but we have Mrs. Finn's
(the wife of Smith's waggoner) unimpeachable
testimony that she saw him get over the low wall of
Hammond's pig-pound and lurch straight at her,
babbling aloud in a voice that was enough to make
one die of fright. Having the baby with her in a
perambulator, Mrs. Finn called out to him to go
away, and as he persisted in coming nearer, she hit

him courageously with her umbrella over the head, and, without once looking back, ran like the wind with the perambulator as far as the first house in the village. She stopped then, out of breath, and spoke to old Lewis, hammering there at a heap of stones; and the old chap, taking off his immense black wire goggles, got up on his shaky legs to look where she pointed. Together they followed with their eyes the figure of the man running over a field; they saw him fall down, pick himself up, and run on again, staggering and waving his long arms above his head, in the direction of the New Barns Farm. From that moment he is plainly in the toils of his obscure and touching destiny. There is no doubt after this of what happened to him. All is certain now: Mrs. Smith's intense terror; Amy Foster's stolid conviction held against the other's nervous attack, that the man ' meant no harm '; Smith's exasperation (on his return from Darnford Market) at finding the dog barking himself into a fit, the back-door locked, his wife in hysterics; and all for an unfortunate dirty tramp, supposed to be even then lurking in his stackyard. Was he? He would teach him to frighten women.

AMY FOSTER

"Smith is notoriously hot-tempered, but the sight of some nondescript and miry creature sitting crosslegged amongst a lot of loose straw, and swinging itself to and fro like a bear in a cage, made him pause. Then this tramp stood up silently before him, one mass of mud and filth from head to foot. Smith, alone amongst his stacks with this apparition, in the stormy twilight ringing with the infuriated barking of the dog, felt the dread of an inexplicable strangeness. But when that being, parting with his black hands the long matted locks that hung before his face, as you part the two halves of a curtain, looked out at him with glistening, wild, black-and-white eyes, the weirdness of this silent encounter fairly staggered him. He had admitted since (for the story has been a legitimate subject of conversation about here for years) that he made more than one step backwards. Then a sudden burst of rapid, senseless speech persuaded him at once that he had to do with an escaped lunatic. In fact, that impression never wore off completely. Smith has not in his heart given up his secret conviction of the man's essential insanity to this very day.

[179]

"As the creature approached him, jabbering in a most discomposing manner, Smith (unaware that he was being addressed as 'gracious lord,' and adjured in God's name to afford food and shelter) kept on speaking firmly but gently to it, and retreating all the time into the other yard. At last, watching his chance, by a sudden charge he bundled him headlong into the wood-lodge, and instantly shot the bolt. Thereupon he wiped his brow, though the day was cold. He had done his duty to the community by shutting up a wandering and probably dangerous maniac. Smith isn't a hard man at all, but he had room in his brain only for that one idea of lunacy. He was not imaginative enough to ask himself whether the man might not be perishing with cold and hunger. Meantime, at first, the maniac made a great deal of noise in the lodge. Mrs. Smith was screaming upstairs, where she had locked herself in her bedroom; but Amy Foster sobbed piteously at the kitchen door, wringing her hands and muttering, 'Don't! don't!' I daresay Smith had a rough time of it that evening with one noise and another, and this insane, disturbing voice crying obstinately through the door only added to his irritation. He couldn't possibly have connected this troublesome lunatic with the sinking of a ship in Eastbay, of which there had been a rumour in the Darnford market-place. And I daresay the man inside had been very near to insanity on that night. Before his excitement collapsed and he became unconscious he was throwing himself violently about in the dark, rolling on some dirty sacks, and biting his fists with rage, cold, hunger, amazement, and despair.

" He was a mountaineer of the eastern range of the Carpathians, and the vessel sunk the night before in Eastbay was the Hamburg emigrant-ship *Herzogin Sophia-Dorothea*, of appalling memory.

" A few months later we could read in the papers the accounts of the bogus ' Emigration Agencies ' among the Sclavonian peasantry in the more remote provinces of Austria. The object of these scoundrels was to get hold of the poor ignorant people's homesteads, and they were in league with the local usurers. They exported their victims through Hamburg mostly. As to the ship, I had watched her out of this very window, reaching close-hauled under short canvas into the bay on a dark, threatening afternoon. She came to an anchor, correctly by the chart, off the Brenzett Coastguard station. I remember before the night fell looking out again at the outlines of her spars and rigging that stood out dark and pointed on a background of ragged, slaty clouds like another and a slighter spire to the left of the Brenzett church-tower. In the evening the wind rose. At midnight I could hear in my bed the terrific gusts and the sounds of a driving deluge.

"About that time the Coastguardmen thought they saw the lights of a steamer over the anchoring-ground. In a moment they vanished; but it is clear that another vessel of some sort had tried for shelter in the bay on that awful, blind night, had rammed the German ship amidships (a breach— as one of the divers told me afterwards—' that you could sail a Thames barge through'), and then had gone out either scathless or damaged, who shall say; but had gone out, unknown, unseen, and fatal, to perish mysteriously at sea. Of her nothing ever came to light, and yet the hue and cry that was raised all over the world would have found her out

[182]

if she had been in existence anywhere on the face of the waters.

"A completeness without a clue, and a stealthy silence as of a neatly executed crime, characterise this murderous disaster, which, as you may remember, had its gruesome celebrity. The wind would have prevented the loudest outcries from reaching the shore; there had been evidently no time for signals of distress. It was death without any sort of fuss. The Hamburg ship, filling all at once, capsized as she sank, and at daylight there was not even the end of a spar to be seen above water. She was missed, of course, and at first the Coastguardmen surmised that she had either dragged her anchor or parted her cable some time during the night, and had been blown out to sea. Then, after the tide turned, the wreck must have shifted a little and released some of the bodies, because a child —a little fair-haired child in a red frock— came ashore abreast of the Martello tower. By the afternoon you could see along three miles of beach dark figures with bare legs dashing in and out of the tumbling foam, and rough-looking men, women with hard faces, children, mostly fair-haired, were being carried, stiff and dripping, on stretchers, on wattles, on ladders, in a long procession past the door of the 'Ship Inn,' to be laid out in a row under the north wall of the Brenzett Church.

" Officially, the body of the little girl in the red frock is the first thing that came ashore from that ship. But I have patients amongst the seafaring population of West Colebrook, and, unofficially, I am informed that very early that morning two brothers, who went down to look after their cobble hauled up on the beach, found, a good way from Brenzett, an ordinary ship's hencoop lying high and dry on the shore, with eleven drowned ducks inside. Their families ate the birds, and the hen-coop was split into firewood with a hatchet. It is possible that a man (supposing he happened to be on deck at the time of the accident) might have floated ashore on that hencoop. He might. I ad-mit it is improbable, but there was the man—and for days, nay, for weeks—it didn't enter our heads that we had amongst us the only living soul that had escaped from that disaster. The man himself, even when he learned to speak intelligibly, could

[184]

tell us very little. He remembered he had felt better (after the ship had anchored, I suppose), and that the darkness, the wind, and the rain took his breath away. This looks as if he had been on deck some time during that night. But we mustn't forget he had been taken out of his knowledge, that he had been sea-sick and battened down below for four days, that he had no general notion of a ship or of the sea, and therefore could have no definite idea of what was happening to him. The rain, the wind, the darkness he knew; he understood the bleating of the sheep, and he remembered the pain of his wretchedness and misery, his heartbroken astonishment that it was neither seen nor understood, his dismay at finding all the men angry and all the women fierce. He had approached them as a beggar, it is true, he said; but in his country, even if they gave nothing, they spoke gently to beggars. The children in his country were not taught to throw stones at those who asked for compassion. Smith's strategy overcame him completely. The wood-lodge presented the horrible aspect of a dungeon. What would be done to him next? . . . No wonder that Amy Foster appeared to his eyes with the aureole of an angel of light. The girl had not been able to sleep for thinking of the poor man, and in the morning, before the Smiths were up, she slipped out across the back yard. Holding the door of the wood-lodge ajar, she looked in and extended to him half a loaf of white bread—' such bread as the rich eat in my country,' he used to say.

" At this he got up slowly from amongst all sorts of rubbish, stiff, hungry, trembling, miserable, and doubtful. ' Can you eat this? ' she asked in her soft and timid voice. He must have taken her for a ' gracious lady.' He devoured ferociously, and tears were falling on the crust. Suddenly he dropped the bread, seized her wrist, and imprinted a kiss on her hand. She was not frightened. Through his forlorn condition she had observed that he was good-looking. She shut the door and walked back slowly to the kitchen. Much later on, she told Mrs. Smith, who shuddered at the bare idea of being touched by that creature.

" Through this act of impulsive pity he was brought back again within the pale of human rela-

tions with his new surroundings. He never forgot
it—never.

"That very same morning old Mr. Swaffer
(Smith's nearest neighbour) came over to give his
advice, and ended by carrying him off. He stood,
unsteady on his legs, meek, and caked over in half-
dried mud, while the two men talked around him in
an incomprehensible tongue. Mrs. Smith had refused to come downstairs till the madman was off
the premises; Amy Foster, far from within the dark
kitchen, watched through the open back door; and
he obeyed the signs that were made to him to the
best of his ability. But Smith was full of mistrust.
' Mind, sir! It may be all his cunning,' he cried
repeatedly in a tone of warning. When Mr.
Swaffer started the mare, the deplorable being sitting humbly by his side, through weakness, nearly
fell out over the back of the high two-wheeled cart.
Swaffer took him straight home. And it is then
that I come upon the scene.

" I was called in by the simple process of the old
man beckoning to me with his forefinger over the
gate of his house as I happened to be driving past.
I got down, of course.

" ' I've got something here,' he mumbled, leading the way to an outhouse at a little distance from his other farm-buildings.

" It was there that I saw him first, in a long low room taken upon the space of that sort of coach-house. It was bare and whitewashed, with a small square aperture glazed with one cracked, dusty pane at its further end. He was lying on his back upon a straw pallet; they had given him a couple of horse-blankets, and he seemed to have spent the remainder of his strength in the exertion of cleaning himself. He was almost speechless; his quick breathing under the blankets pulled up to his chin, his glittering, restless black eyes reminded me of a wild bird caught in a snare. While I was examining him, old Swaffer stood silently by the door, passing the tips of his fingers along his shaven upper lip. I gave some directions, promised to send a bottle of medicine, and naturally made some inquiries.

" ' Smith caught him in the stackyard at New Barns,' said the old chap in his deliberate, unmoved manner, and as if the other had been indeed a sort of wild animal. 'That's how I came by him. Quite a curiosity, isn't he? Now tell me, doctor—

you've been all over the world—don't you think that's a bit of a Hindoo we've got hold of here.'

" I was greatly surprised. His long black hair scattered over the straw bolster contrasted with the olive pallor of his face. It occurred to me he might be a Basque. It didn't necessarily follow that he should understand Spanish; but I tried him with the few words I know, and also with some French. The whispered sounds I caught by bending my ear to his lips puzzled me utterly. That afternoon the young ladies from the Rectory (one of them read Goethe with a dictionary, and the other had struggled with Dante for years), coming to see Miss Swaffer, tried their German and Italian on him from the doorway. They retreated, just the least bit scared by the flood of passionate speech which, turning on his pallet, he let out at them. They admitted that the sound was pleasant, soft, musical— but, in conjunction with his looks perhaps, it was startling—so excitable, so utterly unlike anything one had ever heard. The village boys climbed up the bank to have a peep through the little square aperture. Everybody was wondering what Mr. Swaffer would do with him.

" He simply kept him.

" Swaffer would be called eccentric were he not so much respected. They will tell you that Mr. Swaffer sits up as late as ten o'clock at night to read books, and they will tell you also that he can write a cheque for two hundred pounds without thinking twice about it. He himself would tell you that the Swaffers had owned land between this and Darnford for these three hundred years. He must be eighty-five to-day, but he does not look a bit older than when I first came here. He is a great breeder of sheep, and deals extensively in cattle. He attends market days for miles around in every sort of weather, and drives sitting bowed low over the reins, his lank grey hair curling over the collar of his warm coat, and with a green plaid rug round his legs. The calmness of advanced age gives a solemnity to his manner. He is clean-shaved; his lips are thin and sensitive; something rigid and monachal in the set of his features lends a certain elevation to the character of his face. He has been known to drive miles in the rain to see a new kind of rose in somebody's garden, or a monstrous cabbage grown by a cottager. He loves to

hear tell of or to be shown something that he calls
'outlandish.' Perhaps it was just that outlandish-
ness of the man which influenced old Swaffer. Perhaps it was only an inexplicable caprice. All I
know is that at the end of three weeks I caught
sight of Smith's lunatic digging in Swaffer's kitch-
en garden. They had found out he could use a
spade. He dug barefooted.

"His black hair flowed over his shoulders. I
suppose it was Swaffer who had given him the
striped old cotton shirt; but he wore still the na-
tional brown cloth trousers (in which he had been
washed ashore) fitting to the leg almost like
tights; was belted with a broad leathern belt stud-
ded with little brass discs; and had never yet ventured into the village. The land he looked upon
seemed to him kept neatly, like the grounds round
a landowner's house; the size of the cart-horses
struck him with astonishment; the roads resembled
garden walks, and the aspect of the people, especially on Sundays, spoke of opulence. He wondered what made them so hardhearted and their
children so bold. He got his food at the back door,
carried it in both hands carefully to his outhouse,

and, sitting alone on his pallet, would make the sign of the cross before he began. Beside the same pallet, kneeling in the early darkness of the short days, he recited aloud the Lord's Prayer before he slept. Whenever he saw old Swaffer he would bow with veneration from the waist, and stand erect while the old man, with his fingers over his upper lip, surveyed him silently. He bowed also to Miss Swaffer, who kept house frugally for her father—a broad-shouldered, big-boned woman of forty-five, with the pocket of her dress full of keys, and a grey, steady eye. She was Church—as people said (while her father was one of the trustees of the Baptist Chapel)—and wore a little steel cross at her waist. She dressed severely in black, in memory of one of the innumerable Bradleys of the neighbourhood, to whom she had been engaged some twenty-five years ago—a young farmer who broke his neck out hunting on the eve of the wedding day. She had the unmoved countenance of the deaf, spoke very seldom, and her lips, thin like her father's, astonished one sometimes by a mysteriously ironic curl.

" These were the people to whom he owed allegiance, and an overwhelming loneliness seemed to fall from the leaden sky of that winter without sunshine. All the faces were sad. He could talk to no one, and had no hope of ever understanding anybody. It was as if these had been the faces of people from the other world—dead people—he used to tell me years afterwards. Upon my word, I wonder he did not go mad. He didn't know where he was. Somewhere very far from his mountains—somewhere over the water. Was this America, he wondered?

"If it hadn't been for the steel cross at Miss Swaffer's belt he would not, he confessed, have known whether he was in a Christian country at all. He used to cast stealthy glances at it, and feel comforted. There was nothing here the same as in his country! The earth and the water were different; there were no images of the Redeemer by the roadside. The very grass was different, and the trees. All the trees but the three old Norway pines on the bit of lawn before Swaffer's house, and these reminded him of his country. He had been detected once, after dusk, with his forehead against the trunk of one of them, sobbing, and talking to himself. They had been like brothers to him at that time, he affirmed. Everything else was strange. Conceive you the kind of an existence overshadowed, oppressed, by the everyday material appearances, as if by the visions of a nightmare. At night, when he could not sleep, he kept on thinking of the girl who gave him the first piece of bread he had eaten in this foreign land. She had been neither fierce nor angry, nor frightened. Her face he remembered as the only comprehensible face amongst all these faces that were as closed, as mysterious, and as mute as the faces of the dead who are possessed of a knowledge beyond the comprehension of the living. I wonder whether the memory of her compassion prevented him from cutting his throat. But there! I suppose I am an old sentimentalist, and forget the instinctive love of life which it takes all the strength of an uncommon despair to overcome.

" He did the work which was given him with an intelligence which surprised old Swaffer. By-and-by it was discovered that he could help at the ploughing, could milk the cows, feed the bullocks in the cattle-yard, and was of some use with the sheep. He began to pick up words, too, very fast; and suddenly, one fine morning in spring, he rescued from an untimely death a grand-child of old Swaffer.

" Swaffer's younger daughter is married to Willcox, a solicitor and the Town Clerk of Colebrook. Regularly twice a year they come to stay with the old man for a few days. Their only child, a little girl not three years old at the time, ran out of the house alone in her little white pinafore, and, toddling across the grass of a terraced garden, pitched herself over a low wall head first into the horsepond in the yard below.

" Our man was out with the waggoner and the plough in the field nearest to the house, and as he was leading the team round to begin a fresh furrow, he saw, through the gap of the gate, what for anybody else would have been a mere flutter of something white. But he had straight-glancing, quick, far-reaching eyes, that only seemed to flinch and lose their amazing power before the immensity of the sea. He was barefooted, and looking as outlandish as the heart of Swaffer could desire. Leaving the horses on the turn, to the inexpressible disgust of the waggoner he bounded off, going over the ploughed ground in long leaps, and suddenly appeared before the mother, thrust the child into her arms, and strode away.

" The pond was not very deep; but still, if he had not had such good eyes, the child would have perished—miserably suffocated in the foot or so of sticky mud at the bottom. Old Swaffer walked out slowly into the field, waited till the plough came over to his side, had a good look at him, and without saying a word went back to the house. But from that time they laid out his meals on the kitchen table; and at first, Miss Swaffer, all in black and with an inscrutable face, would come and stand in the doorway of the living-room to see him make a big sign of the cross before he fell to. I believe that from that day, too, Swaffer began to pay him regular wages.

" I can't follow step by step his development. He cut his hair short, was seen in the village and along the road going to and fro to his work like any other man. Children ceased to shout after him. He became aware of social differences, but remained for a long time surprised at the bare poverty of the churches among so much wealth. He couldn't understand either why they were kept shut up on week days. There was nothing to steal in them. Was it to keep people from praying too often? The rectory took much notice of him about that time, and I believe the young ladies attempted to prepare the ground for his conversion. They could not, however, break him of his habit of crossing himself, but he went so far as to take off the string with a couple of brass medals the size of a sixpence, a tiny metal cross, and a square sort of scapulary which he wore round his neck. He hung them on the wall by the side of his bed, and he was still to be heard every evening reciting the Lord's Prayer, in incomprehensible words and in a slow, fervent tone, as he had heard his old father do at the head of all the kneeling family, big and little, on every evening of his life. And though he wore corduroys at work, and a slop-made pepper-and-salt suit on Sundays, strangers would turn round to look after him on the road. His foreignness had a peculiar and indelible stamp. At last people became used to see him. But they never became used to him. His rapid, skimming walk; his swarthy

[197]

complexion; his hat cocked on the left ear; his habit, on warm evenings, of wearing his coat over one shoulder, like a hussar's dolman; his manner of leaping over the stiles, not as a feat of agility, but in the ordinary course of progression—all these peculiarities were, as one may say, so many causes of scorn and offence to the inhabitants of the village. *They* wouldn't in their dinner hour lie flat on their backs on the grass to stare at the sky. Neither did they go about the fields screaming dismal tunes. Many times have I heard his high-pitched voice from behind the ridge of some sloping sheep-walk, a voice light and soaring, like a lark's, but with a melancholy human note, over our fields that hear only the song of birds. And I should be startled myself. Ah! He was different: innocent of heart, and full of good will, which nobody wanted, this castaway, that, like a man transplanted into another planet, was separated by an immense space from his past and by an immense ignorance from his future. His quick, fervent utterance positively shocked everybody. 'An excitable devil,' they called him. One evening, in the tap-room of the Coach and Horses (having drunk some whisky), he upset them all by singing a love song of his country. They hooted him down, and he was pained; but Preble, the lame wheelwright, and Vincent, the fat blacksmith, and the other notables too, wanted to drink their evening beer in peace. On another occasion he tried to show them how to dance. The dust rose in clouds from the sanded floor; he leaped straight up amongst the deal tables, struck his heels together, squatted on one heel in front of old Preble, shooting out the other leg, uttered wild and exulting cries, jumped up to whirl on one foot, snapping his fingers above his head—and a strange carter who was having a drink in there began to swear, and cleared out with his half-pint in his hand into the bar. But when suddenly he sprang upon a table and continued to dance among the glasses, the landlord interfered. He didn't want any ' accrobat tricks in the tap-room.' They laid their hands on him. Having had a glass or two, Mr. Swaffer's foreigner tried to expostulate: was ejected forcibly: got a black eye.

" I believe he felt the hostility of his human surroundings. But he was tough—tough in spirit, too, as well as in body. Only the memory of the sea frightened him, with that vague terror that is left by a bad dream. His home was far away; and he did not want now to go to America. I had often explained to him that there is no place on earth where true gold can be found lying ready and to be got for the trouble of the picking up. How then, he asked, could he ever return home with empty hands when there had been sold a cow, two ponies, and a bit of land to pay for his going? His eyes would fill with tears, and, averting them from the immense shimmer of the sea, he would throw himself face down on the grass. But sometimes, cocking his hat with a little conquering air, he would defy my wisdom. He had found his bit of true gold. That was Amy Foster's heart; which was ' a golden heart, and soft to people's misery,' he would say in the accents of overwhelming conviction.

" He was called Yanko. He had explained that this meant little John; but as he would also repeat very often that he was a mountaineer (some word sounding in the dialect of his country like Goorall) he got it for his surname. And this is the only trace of him that the succeeding ages may find in the marriage register of the parish. There it stands—Yanko Goorall—in the rector's handwriting. The crooked cross made by the castaway, a cross whose tracing no doubt seemed to him the most solemn part of the whole ceremony, is all that remains now to perpetuate the memory of his name.

" His courtship had lasted some time—ever since he got his precarious footing in the community. It began by his buying for Amy Foster a green satin ribbon in Darnford. This was what you did in his country. You bought a ribbon at a Jew's stall on a fair-day. I don't suppose the girl knew what to do with it, but he seemed to think that his honourable intentions could not be mistaken.

" It was only when he declared his purpose to get married that I fully understood how, for a hundred futile and inappreciable reasons, how—shall I say odious?—he was to all the countryside. Every old woman in the village was up in arms. Smith, coming upon him near the farm, promised to break his head for him if he found him about again. But he twisted his little black moustache with such a bellicose air and rolled such big, black

[201]

fierce eyes at Smith that this promise came to nothing. Smith, however, told the girl that she must be mad to take up with a man who was surely wrong in his head. All the same, when she heard him in the gloaming whistle from beyond the orchard a couple of bars of a weird and mournful tune, she would drop whatever she had in her hand—she would leave Mrs. Smith in the middle of a sentence —and she would run out to his call. Mrs. Smith called her a shameless hussy. She answered nothing. She said nothing at all to anybody, and went on her way as if she had been deaf. She and I alone all in the land, I fancy, could see his very real beauty. He was very good-looking, and most graceful in his bearing, with that something wild as of a woodland creature in his aspect. Her mother moaned over her dismally whenever the girl came to see her on her day out. The father was surly, but pretended not to know; and Mrs. Finn once told her plainly that ' this man, my dear, will do you some harm some day yet.' And so it went on. They could be seen on the roads, she tramping stolidly in her finery—grey dress, black feather, stout boots, prominent white cotton gloves that caught your eye a hundred yards away; and he, his coat slung picturesquely over one shoulder, pacing by her side, gallant of bearing and casting tender glances upon the girl with the golden heart. I wonder whether he saw how plain she was. Perhaps among types so different from what he had ever seen, he had not the power to judge; or perhaps he was seduced by the divine quality of her pity.

"Yanko was in great trouble meantime. In his country you get an old man for an ambassador in marriage affairs. He did not know how to proceed. However, one day in the midst of sheep in a field (he was now Swaffer's under-shepherd with Foster) he took off his hat to the father and declared himself humbly. 'I daresay she's fool enough to marry you,' was all Foster said. 'And then,' he used to relate, 'he puts his hat on his head, looks black at me as if he wanted to cut my throat, whistles the dog, and off he goes, leaving me to do the work.' The Fosters, of course, didn't like to lose the wages the girl earned: Amy used to give all her money to her mother. But there was in Foster a very genuine aversion to that match. He con-

[203]

tended that the fellow was very good with sheep,
but was not fit for any girl to marry. For one
thing, he used to go along the hedges muttering to
himself like a dam' fool; and then, these foreign-
ers behave very queerly to women sometimes. And
perhaps he would want to carry her off somewhere
—or run off himself. It was not safe. He
preached it to his daughter that the fellow might
ill-use her in some way. She made no answer. It
was, they said in the village, as if the man had done
something to her. People discussed the matter. It
was quite an excitement, and the two went on
' walking out ' together in the face of opposition.
Then something unexpected happened.

" I don't know whether old Swaffer ever understood how much he was regarded in the light of a
father by his foreign retainer. Anyway the rela-
tion was curiously feudal. So when Yanko asked
formally for an interview—' and the Miss too ' (he
called the severe, deaf Miss Swaffer simply *Miss*)
—it was to obtain their permission to marry.
Swaffer heard him unmoved, dismissed him by a
nod, and then shouted the intelligence into Miss
Swaffer's best ear. She showed no surprise, and

only remarked grimly, in a veiled blank voice, ' He certainly won't get any other girl to marry him.'

" It is Miss Swaffer who has all the credit of the munificence: but in a very few days it came out that Mr. Swaffer had presented Yanko with a cottage (the cottage you've seen this morning) and something like an acre of ground—had made it over to him in absolute property. Willcox expedited the deed, and I remember him telling me he had a great pleasure in making it ready. It recited: ' In consideration of saving the life of my beloved grandchild, Bertha Willcox.'

" Of course, after that no power on earth could prevent them from getting married.

" Her infatuation endured. People saw her going out to meet him in the evening, she standing with unblinking, fascinated eyes up the road where he was expected to appear, walking freely, with a swing from the hip, and humming one of the love-tunes of his country. When the boy was born, he got elevated at the ' Coach and Horses,' essayed again a song and a dance, and was again ejected. People expressed their commiseration for a woman married to that Jack-in-the-box. He didn't care.

There was a man now (he told me boastfully) to whom he could sing and talk in the language of his country, and show how to dance by-and-by.

" But I don't know. To me he appeared to have grown less springy of step, heavier in body, less keen of eye. Imagination, no doubt; but it seems to me now as if the net of fate had been drawn closer round him already.

" One day I met him on the footpath over the Talfourd Hill. He told me that ' women were funny.' I had heard already of domestic differences. People were saying that Amy Foster was beginning to find out what sort of man she had married. He looked upon the sea with indifferent, unseeing eyes. His wife had snatched the child out of his arms one day as he sat on the doorstep crooning to it a song such as the mothers sing to babies in his mountains. She seemed to think he was doing it some harm. Women are funny. And she had objected to him praying aloud in the evening. Why? He expected the boy to repeat the prayer aloud after him by-and-by, as he used to do after his old father when he was a child—in his own country. And I discovered he longed for their boy to grow

up so that he could have a man to talk with in that
language that to our ears sounded so disturbing,
so passionate, and so bizarre. Why his wife
should dislike the idea he couldn't tell. But that
would pass, he said. And tilting his head know-
ingly, he tapped his breastbone to indicate that she
had a good heart: not hard, not fierce, open to compassion, charitable to the poor!

"I walked away thoughtfully; I wondered
whether his difference, his strangeness, were not
penetrating with repulsion that dull nature they
had begun by irresistibly attracting. I wondered. . . ."

The Doctor came to the window and looked out
at the frigid splendour of the sea, immense in
the haze, as if enclosing all the earth with all
the hearts lost among the passions of love and
fear.

"Physiologically, now," he said, turning away
abruptly, "it was possible. It was possible."

He remained silent. Then went on—

"At all events, the next time I saw him he was
ill—lung trouble. He was tough, but I daresay he
was not acclimatised as well as I had supposed. It

was a bad winter; and, of course, these mountain-
eers do get fits of home sickness; and a state of depression would make him vulnerable. He was lying
half dressed on a couch downstairs.

"A table covered with a dark oilcloth took up all
the middle of the little room. There was a wicker
cradle on the floor, a kettle spouting steam on the
hob, and some child's linen lay drying on the
fender. The room was warm, but the door opens
right into the garden, as you noticed perhaps.

"He was very feverish, and kept on muttering
to himself. She sat on a chair and looked at him
fixedly across the table with her brown, blurred
eyes. 'Why don't you have him upstairs?' I
asked. With a start and a confused stammer she
said, 'Oh! ah! I couldn't sit with him upstairs,
Sir.'

"I gave her certain directions; and going outside, I said again that he ought to be in bed upstairs. She wrung her hands. 'I couldn't. I
couldn't. He keeps on saying something—I don't
know what.' With the memory of all the talk
against the man that had been dinned into her ears,
I looked at her narrowly. I looked into her short-

sighted eyes, at her dumb eyes that once in her life had seen an enticing shape, but seemed, staring at me, to see nothing at all now. But I saw she was uneasy.

" ' What's the matter with him? ' she asked in a sort of vacant trepidation. ' He doesn't look very ill. I never did see anybody look like this before. . . .'

" ' Do you think,' I asked indignantly, ' he is shamming? '

" ' I can't help it, sir,' she said stolidly. And suddenly she clapped her hands and looked right and left. ' And there's the baby. I am so frightened. He wanted me just now to give him the baby. I can't understand what he says to it.'

" ' Can't you ask a neighbour to come in to-night? ' I asked.

" ' Please, sir, nobody seems to care to come,' she muttered, dully resigned all at once.

" I impressed upon her the necessity of the greatest care, and then had to go. There was a good deal of sickness that winter. ' Oh, I hope he won't talk! ' she exclaimed softly just as I was going away.

"I don't know how it is I did not see—but I didn't. And yet, turning in my trap, I saw her lingering before the door, very still, and as if meditating a flight up the miry road.

"Towards the night his fever increased.

"He tossed, moaned, and now and then muttered a complaint. And she sat with the table between her and the couch, watching every movement and every sound, with the terror, the unreasonable terror, of that man she could not understand creeping over her. She had drawn the wicker cradle close to her feet. There was nothing in her now but the maternal instinct and that unaccountable fear.

"Suddenly coming to himself, parched, he demanded a drink of water. She did not move. She had not understood, though he may have thought he was speaking in English. He waited, looking at her, burning with fever, amazed at her silence and immobility, and then he shouted impatiently, 'Water! Give me water!'

"She jumped to her feet, snatched up the child, and stood still. He spoke to her, and his passionate remonstrances only increased her fear of that strange man. I believe he spoke to her for a long

[210]

time, entreating, wondering, pleading, ordering, I suppose. She says she bore it as long as she could. And then a gust of rage came over him.

"He sat up and called out terribly one word—some word. Then he got up as though he hadn't been ill at all, she says. And as in fevered dismay, indignation, and wonder he tried to get to her round the table, she simply opened the door and ran out with the child in her arms. She heard him call twice after her down the road in a terrible voice—and fled. . . . Ah! but you should have seen stirring behind the dull, blurred glance of these eyes the spectre of the fear which had hunted her on that night three miles and a half to the door of Foster's cottage! I did the next day.

"And it was I who found him lying face down and his body in a puddle, just outside the little wicker-gate.

"I had been called out that night to an urgent case in the village, and on my way home at daybreak passed by the cottage. The door stood open. My man helped me to carry him in. We laid him on the couch. The lamp smoked, the fire was out, the chill of the stormy night oozed from the cheerless yellow paper on the wall. 'Amy!' I called aloud, and my voice seemed to lose itself in the emptiness of this tiny house as if I had cried in a desert. He opened his eyes. 'Gone!' he said distinctly. 'I had only asked for water—only for a little water. . . .'

"He was muddy. I covered him up and stood waiting in silence, catching a painfully gasped word now and then. They were no longer in his own language. The fever had left him, taking with it the heat of life. And with his panting breast and lustrous eyes he reminded me again of a wild creature under the net; of a bird caught in a snare. She had left him. She had left him—sick —helpless—thirsty. The spear of the hunter had entered his very soul. 'Why?' he cried in the penetrating and indignant voice of a man calling to a responsible Maker. A gust of wind and a swish of rain answered.

"And as I turned away to shut the door he pronounced the word 'Merciful!' and expired.

"Eventually I certified heart-failure as the immediate cause of death. His heart must have indeed failed him, or else he might have stood this night of storm and exposure, too. I closed his eyes and drove away. Not very far from the cottage I met Foster walking sturdily between the dripping hedges with his collie at his heels.

" ' Do you know where your daughter is? ' I asked.

" ' Don't I ! ' he cried. ' I am going to talk to him a bit. Frightening a poor woman like this.'

" ' He won't frighten her any more,' I said. ' He is dead.'

" He struck with his stick at the mud.

" ' And there's the child.'

" Then, after thinking deeply for a while—

" ' I don't know that it isn't for the best.'

" That's what he said. And she says nothing at all now. Not a word of him. Never. Is his image as utterly gone from her mind as his lithe and striding figure, his carolling voice are gone from our fields? He is no longer before her eyes to excite her imagination into a passion of love or fear ; and his memory seems to have vanished from her dull brain as a shadow passes away upon a white screen. She lives in the cottage and works for Miss Swaffer. She is Amy Foster for everybody, and the child is 'Amy Foster's boy.' She calls him Johnny—which means Little John.

"It is impossible to say whether this name recalls anything to her. Does she ever think of the past? I have seen her hanging over the boy's cot in a very passion of maternal tenderness. The little fellow was lying on his back, a little frightened at me, but very still, with his big black eyes, with his fluttered air of a bird in a snare. And looking at him I seemed to see again the other one—the father, cast out mysteriously by the sea to perish in the supreme disaster of loneliness and despair."

TO-MORROW

TO-MORROW

What was known of Captain Hagberd in the little seaport of Colebrook was not exactly in his favour. He did not belong to the place. He had come to settle there under circumstances not at all mysterious—he used to be very communicative about them at the time—but extremely morbid and unreasonable. He was possessed of some little money evidently, because he bought a plot of ground, and had a pair of ugly yellow brick cottages run up very cheaply. He occupied one of them himself and let the other to Josiah Carvil—blind Carvil, the retired boat-builder—a man of evil repute as a domestic tyrant.

These cottages had one wall in common, shared in a line of iron railing dividing their front gardens; a wooden fence separated their back gardens. Miss Bessie Carvil was allowed, as it were of right, to throw over it the tea-cloths, blue rags, or an apron that wanted drying.

[217]

"It rots the wood, Bessie my girl," the captain would remark mildly, from his side of the fence, each time he saw her exercising that privilege.

She was a tall girl; the fence was low, and she could spread her elbows on the top. Her hands would be red with the bit of washing she had done, but her forearms were white and shapely, and she would look at her father's landlord in silence—in an informed silence which had an air of knowledge, expectation and desire.

"It rots the wood," repeated Captain Hagberd. "It is the only unthrifty, careless habit I know in you. Why don't you have a clothes line out in your back yard?"

Miss Carvil would say nothing to this—she only shook her head negatively. The tiny back yard on her side had a few stone-bordered little beds of black earth, in which the simple flowers she found time to cultivate appeared somehow extravagantly overgrown, as if belonging to an exotic clime; and Captain Hagberd's upright, hale person, clad in No. 1 sail-cloth from head to foot, would be emerging knee-deep out of rank grass and the tall weeds on his side of the fence. He appeared, with the col-

our and uncouth stiffness of the extraordinary material in which he chose to clothe himself—" for the
time being," would be his mumbled remark to any
observation on the subject—like a man roughened
out of granite, standing in a wilderness not big
enough for a decent billiard-room. A heavy figure
of a man of stone, with a red handsome face, a blue
wandering eye, and a great white beard flowing
to his waist and never trimmed as far as Colebrook
knew.

Seven years before, he had seriously answered,
" Next month, I think," to the chaffing attempt to
secure his custom made by that distinguished local
wit, the Colebrook barber, who happened to be sitting insolently in the tap-room of the New Inn near
the harbour, where the captain had entered to buy
an ounce of tobacco. After paying for his pur-
chase with three half-pence extracted from the corner of a handkerchief which he carried in the cuff
of his sleeve, Captain Hagberd went out. As soon
as the door was shut the barber laughed. " The
old one and the young one will be strolling arm in
arm to get shaved in my place presently. The
tailor shall be set to work, and the barber, and the

candlestick maker; high old times are coming for Colebrook, they are coming, to be sure. It used to be ' next week,' now it has come to ' next month,' and so on—soon it will be next spring, for all I know."

Noticing a stranger listening to him with a vacant grin, he explained, stretching out his legs cynically, that this queer old Hagberd, a retired coasting-skipper, was waiting for the return of a son of his. The boy had been driven away from home, he shouldn't wonder; had run away to sea and had never been heard of since. Put to rest in Davy Jones's locker this many a day, as likely as not. That old man came flying to Colebrook three years ago all in black broadcloth (had lost his wife lately then), getting out of a third-class smoker as if the devil had been at his heels; and the only thing that brought him down was a letter—a hoax probably. Some joker had written to him about a seafaring man with some such name who was supposed to be hanging about some girl or other, either in Colebrook or in the neighbourhood. "Funny, ain't it?" The old chap had been advertising in the London papers for Harry Hagberd, and offering rewards for any sort of likely information. And the barber would go on to describe with sardonic gusto, how that stranger in mourning had been seen exploring the country, in carts, on foot, taking everybody into his confidence, visiting all the inns and alehouses for miles around, stopping people on the road with his questions, looking into the very ditches almost; first in the greatest excitement, then with a plodding sort of perseverance, growing slower and slower; and he could not even tell you plainly how his son looked. The sailor was supposed to be one of two that had left a timber ship, and to have been seen dangling after some girl; but the old man described a boy of fourteen or so—" a clever-looking, high-spirited boy." And when people only smiled at this he would rub his forehead in a confused sort of way before he slunk off, looking offended. He found nobody, of course; not a trace of anybody—never heard of anything worth belief, at any rate; but he had not been able somehow to tear himself away from Colebrook.

" It was the shock of this disappointment, perhaps, coming soon after the loss of his wife, that had driven him crazy on that point," the barber suggested, with an air of great psychological insight. After a time the old man abandoned the active search. His son had evidently gone away; but he settled himself to wait. His son had been once at least in Colebrook in preference to his native place. There must have been some reason for it, he seemed to think, some very powerful inducement, that would bring him back to Colebrook again.

"Ha, ha, ha! Why, of course, Colebrook. Where else? That's the only place in the United Kingdom for your long-lost sons. So he sold up his old home in Colchester, and down he comes here. Well, it's a craze, like any other. Wouldn't catch me going crazy over any of my youngsters clearing out. I've got eight of them at home." The barber was showing off his strength of mind in the midst of a laughter that shook the tap-room.

Strange, though, that sort of thing, he would confess, with the frankness of a superior intelligence, seemed to be catching. His establishment, for instance, was near the harbour, and whenever a sailorman came in for a hair-cut or a shave—if it

[222]

was a strange face he couldn't help thinking directly, "Suppose he's the son of old Hagberd!" He laughed at himself for it. It was a strong craze. He could remember the time when the whole town was full of it. But he had his hopes of the old chap yet. He would cure him by a course of judicious chaffing. He was watching the progress of the treatment. Next week—next month—next year! When the old skipper had put off the date of that return till next year, he would be well on his way to not saying any more about it. In other matters he was quite rational, so this, too, was bound to come. Such was the barber's firm opinion.

Nobody had ever contradicted him; his own hair had gone grey since that time, and Captain Hagberd's beard had turned quite white, and had acquired a majestic flow over the No. 1 canvas suit, which he had made for himself secretly with tarred twine, and had assumed suddenly, coming out in it one fine morning, whereas the evening before he had been seen going home in his mourning of broadcloth. It caused a sensation in the High Street—shopkeepers coming to their doors, people

[223]

in the houses snatching up their hats to run out—
a stir at which he seemed strangely surprised at
first, and then scared; but his only answer to the
wondering questions was that startled and evasive,
" For the present."

That sensation had been forgotten, long ago;
and Captain Hagberd himself, if not forgotten,
had come to be disregarded—the penalty of daili-
ness—as the sun itself is disregarded unless it
makes its power felt heavily. Captain Hagberd's
movements showed no infirmity: he walked stiffly
in his suit of canvas, a quaint and remarkable figure; only his eyes wandered more furtively perhaps
than of yore. His manner abroad had lost its excitable watchfulness; it had become puzzled and
diffident, as though he had suspected that there
was somewhere about him something slightly com-
promising, some embarrassing oddity; and yet had
remained unable to discover what on earth this
something wrong could be.

He was unwilling now to talk with the townsfolk.
He had earned for himself the reputation of an
awful skinflint, of a miser in the matter of living.
He mumbled regretfully in the shops, bought in-

ferior scraps of meat after long hesitations; and discouraged all allusions to his costume. It was as the barber had foretold. For all one could tell, he had recovered already from the disease of hope; and only Miss Bessie Carvil knew that he said nothing about his son's return because with him it was no longer " next week," " next month," or even " next year." It was " to-morrow."

In their intimacy of back yard and front garden he talked with her paternally, reasonably, and dogmatically, with a touch of arbitrariness. They met on the ground of unreserved confidence, which was authenticated by an affectionate wink now and then. Miss Carvil had come to look forward rather to these winks. At first they had discomposed her: the poor fellow was mad. Afterwards she had learned to laugh at them: there was no harm in him. Now she was aware of an unacknowledged, pleasurable, incredulous emotion, expressed by a faint blush. He winked not in the least vulgarly; his thin red face with a well-modelled curved nose, had a sort of distinction—the more so that when he talked to her he looked with a steadier and more intelligent glance. A handsome, hale, upright, ca-

pable man, with a white beard. You did not think
of his age. His son, he affirmed, had resembled
him amazingly from his earliest babyhood.

Harry would be one-and-thirty next July, he
declared. Proper age to get married with a nice,
sensible girl that could appreciate a good home.
He was a very high-spirited boy. High-spirited
husbands were the easiest to manage. These mean,
soft chaps, that you would think butter wouldn't
melt in their mouths, were the ones to make a woman thoroughly miserable. And there was nothing
like a home—a fireside—a good roof: no turning
out of your warm bed in all sorts of weather. " Eh,
my dear? "

Captain Hagberd had been one of those sailors
that pursue their calling within sight of land. One
of the many children of a bankrupt farmer, he had
been apprenticed hurriedly to a coasting skipper,
and had remained on the coast all his sea life. It
must have been a hard one at first: he had never
taken to it; his affection turned to the land, with
its innumerable houses, with its quiet lives gathered
round its firesides. Many sailors feel and profess
a rational dislike for the sea, but his was a pro-

found and emotional animosity—as if the love of
the stabler element had been bred into him through
many generations.

" People did not know what they let their boys in
for when they let them go to sea," he expounded to
Bessie. " As soon make convicts of them at once."
He did not believe you ever got used to it. The
weariness of such a life got worse as you got older.
What sort of trade was it in which more than half
your time you did not put your foot inside your
house? Directly you got out to sea you had no
means of knowing what went on at home. One
might have thought him weary of distant voyages;
and the longest he had ever made had lasted a fortnight, of which the most part had been spent at
anchor, sheltering from the weather. As soon as
his wife had inherited a house and enough to live on
(from a bachelor uncle who had made some money
in the coal business) he threw up his command of
an East-coast collier with a feeling as though he
had escaped from the galleys. After all these years
he might have counted on the fingers of his two
hands all the days he had been out of sight of England. He had never known what it was to be out

of soundings. " I have never been further than eighty fathoms from the land," was one of his boasts.

Bessie Carvil heard all these things. In front of their cottage grew an under-sized ash; and on summer afternoons she would bring out a chair on the grass-plot and sit down with her sewing. Captain Hagberd, in his canvas suit, leaned on a spade. He dug every day in his front plot. He turned it over and over several times every year, but was not going to plant anything " just at present."

To Bessie Carvil he would state more explicitly : " Not till our Harry comes home to-morrow." And she had heard this formula of hope so often that it only awakened the vaguest pity in her heart for that hopeful old man.

Everything was put off in that way, and everything was being prepared likewise for to-morrow. There was a boxful of packets of various flowerseeds to choose from, for the front garden. " He will doubtless let you have your say about that, my dear," Captain Hagberd intimated to her across the railing.

[228]

Miss Bessie's head remained bowed over her
work. She had heard all this so many times. But
now and then she would rise, lay down her sewing,
and come slowly to the fence. There was a charm
in these gentle ravings. He was determined that
his son should not go away again for the want of a
home all ready for him. He had been filling the
other cottage with all sorts of furniture. She imagined it all new, fresh with varnish, piled up as
in a warehouse. There would be tables wrapped
up in sacking; rolls of carpets thick and vertical
like fragments of columns, the gleam of white marble tops in the dimness of the drawn blinds. Captain Hagberd always described his purchases to
her, carefully, as to a person having a legitimate
interest in them. The overgrown yard of his cottage could be laid over with concrete . . . after
to-morrow.

"We may just as well do away with the fence.
You could have your drying-line out, quite clear of
your flowers." He winked, and she would blush
faintly.

This madness that had entered her life through
the kind impulses of her heart had reasonable de-

tails. What if some day his son returned? But she could not even be quite sure that he ever had a son; and if he existed anywhere he had been too long away. When Captain Hagberd got excited in his talk she would steady him by a pretence of belief, laughing a little to salve her conscience.

Only once she had tried pityingly to throw some doubt on that hope doomed to disappointment, but the effect of her attempt had scared her very much. All at once over that man's face there came an expression of horror and incredulity, as though he had seen a crack open out in the firmament.

" You—you—you don't think he's drowned!"

For a moment he seemed to her ready to go out of his mind, for in his ordinary state she thought him more sane than people gave him credit for. On that occasion the violence of the emotion was followed by a most paternal and complacent recovery.

" Don't alarm yourself, my dear," he said a little cunningly: " the sea can't keep him. He does not belong to it. None of us Hagberds ever did belong to it. Look at me; I didn't get drowned. Moreover, he isn't a sailor at all; and if he is not a sailor he's bound to come back. There's nothing to prevent him coming back. . . ."

His eyes began to wander.

" To-morrow."

She never tried again, for fear the man should go out of his mind on the spot. He depended on her. She seemed the only sensible person in the town; and he would congratulate himself frankly before her face on having secured such a level-headed wife for his son. The rest of the town, he confided to her once, in a fit of temper, was certainly queer. The way they looked at you—the way they talked to you! He had never got on with any one in the place. Didn't like the people. He would not have left his own country if it had not been clear that his son had taken a fancy to Colebrook.

She humoured him in silence, listening patiently by the fence; crocheting with downcast eyes. Blushes came with difficulty on her dead-white complexion, under the negligently twisted opulence of mahogany-coloured hair. Her father was frankly carroty.

She had a full figure; a tired, unrefreshed face. When Captain Hagberd vaunted the necessity and propriety of a home and the delights of one's own fireside, she smiled a little, with her lips only. Her home delights had been confined to the nursing of her father during the ten best years of her life.

A bestial roaring coming out of an upstairs window would interrupt their talk. She would begin at once to roll up her crochet-work or fold her sewing, without the slightest sign of haste. Meanwhile the howls and roars of her name would go on, making the fishermen strolling upon the sea-wall on the other side of the road turn their heads towards the cottages. She would go in slowly at the front door, and a moment afterwards there would fall a profound silence. Presently she would reappear, leading by the hand a man, gross and unwieldy like a hippopotamus, with a bad-tempered, surly face.

He was a widowed boat-builder, whom blindness had overtaken years before in the full flush of business. He behaved to his daughter as if she had been responsible for its incurable character. He had been heard to bellow at the top of his voice, as if to defy Heaven, that he did not care: he had made enough money to have ham and eggs for his breakfast every morning. He thanked God for it, in a fiendish tone as though he were cursing.

Captain Hagberd had been so unfavourably impressed by his tenant, that once he told Miss Bessie, " He is a very extravagant fellow, my dear."

She was knitting that day, finishing a pair of socks for her father, who expected her to keep up the supply dutifully. She hated knitting, and, as she was just at the heel part, she had to keep her eyes on her needles.

" Of course it isn't as if he had a son to provide for," Captain Hagberd went on a little vacantly. " Girls, of course, don't require so much—h'm—h'm. They don't run away from home, my dear."

" No," said Miss Bessie, quietly.

Captain Hagberd, amongst the mounds of turned-up earth, chuckled. With his maritime rig, his weather-beaten face, his beard of Father Neptune, he resembled a deposed sea-god who had exchanged the trident for the spade.

" And he must look upon you as already provided for, in a manner. That's the best of it with the girls. The husbands . . ." He winked. Miss Bessie, absorbed in her knitting, coloured faintly.

[233]

"Bessie! my hat!" old Carvil bellowed out suddenly. He had been sitting under the tree mute and motionless, like an idol of some remarkably monstrous superstition. He never opened his mouth but to howl for her, at her, sometimes about her; and then he did not moderate the terms of his abuse. Her system was never to answer him at all; and he kept up his shouting till he got attended to —till she shook him by the arm, or thrust the mouthpiece of his pipe between his teeth. He was one of the few blind people who smoke. When he felt the hat being put on his head he stopped his noise at once. Then he rose, and they passed together through the gate.

He weighed heavily on her arm. During their slow, toilful walks she appeared to be dragging with her for a penance the burden of that infirm bulk. Usually they crossed the road at once (the cottages stood in the fields near the harbour, two hundred yards away from the end of the. street), and for a long, long time they would remain in view, ascending imperceptibly the flight of wooden steps that led to the top of the sea-wall. It ran on from east to west, shutting out the Channel like

[234]

a neglected railway embankment, on which no train had ever rolled within memory of man. Groups of sturdy fishermen would emerge upon the sky, walk along for a bit, and sink without haste. Their brown nets, like the cobwebs of gigantic spiders, lay on the shabby grass of the slope; and, looking up from the end of the street, the people of the town would recognise the two Carvils by the creeping slowness of their gait. Captain Hagberd, pottering aimlessly about his cottages, would raise his head to see how they got on in their promenade.

He advertised still in the Sunday papers for Harry Hagberd. These sheets were read in foreign parts to the end of the world, he informed Bessie. At the same time he seemed to think that his son was in England—so near to Colebrook that he would of course turn up " to-morrow." Bessie, without committing herself to that opinion in so many words, argued that in that case the expense of advertising was unnecessary; Captain Hagberd had better spend that weekly half-crown on himself. She declared she did not know what he lived on. Her argumentation would puzzle him and cast him down for a time. "They all do it," he pointed out. There was a whole column devoted to appeals after missing relatives. He would bring the newspaper to show her. He and his wife had advertised for years; only she was an impatient woman. The news from Colebrook had arrived the very day after her funeral; if she had not been so impatient she might have been here now, with no more than one day more to wait. "You are not an impatient woman, my dear."

"I've no patience with you sometimes," she would say.

If he still advertised for his son he did not offer rewards for information any more; for, with the muddled lucidity of a mental derangement he had reasoned himself into a conviction as clear as daylight that he had already attained all that could be expected in that way. What more could he want? Colebrook was the place, and there was no need to ask for more. Miss Carvil praised him for his good sense, and he was soothed by the part she took in his hope, which had become his delusion; in that idea which blinded his mind to truth and probability, just as the other old man in the other cottage had been made blind, by another disease, to the light and beauty of the world.

But anything he could interpret as a doubt— any coldness of assent, or even a simple inattention to the development of his projects of a home with his returned son and his son's wife—would irritate him into flings and jerks and wicked side glances. He would dash his spade into the ground and walk to and fro before it. Miss Bessie called it his tantrums. She shook her finger at him. Then, when she came out again, after he had parted with her in anger, he would watch out of the corner of his eyes for the least sign of encouragement to approach the iron railings and resume his fatherly and patronising relations.

For all their intimacy, which had lasted some years now, they had never talked without a fence or a railing between them. He described to her all the splendours accumulated for the setting-up of their housekeeping, but had never invited her to an inspection. No human eye was to behold them till Harry had his first look. In fact, nobody had ever been inside his cottage; he did his own housework, and he guarded his son's privilege so jealously that

the small objects of domestic use he bought sometimes in the town were smuggled rapidly across the
front garden under his canvas coat. Then, coming
out, he would remark apologetically, " It was only
a small kettle, my dear."

And, if not too tired with her drudgery, or wor-
ried beyond endurance by her father, she would
laugh at him with a blush, and say: " That's all
right, Captain Hagberd; I am not impatient."

" Well, my dear, you haven't long to wait now,"
he would answer with a sudden bashfulness, and
looking uneasily, as though he had suspected that
there was something wrong somewhere.

Every Monday she paid him his rent over the
railings. He clutched the shillings greedily. He
grudged every penny he had to spend on his main-
tenance, and when he left her to make his purchases
his bearing changed as soon as he got into the
street. Away from the sanction of her pity, he felt
himself exposed without defence. He brushed the
walls with his shoulder. He mistrusted the queer-
ness of the people; yet, by then, even the town
children had left off calling after him, and the
tradesmen served him without a word. The slight-

[238]

est allusion to his clothing had the power to puzzle and frighten especially, as if it were something utterly unwarranted and incomprehensible.

In the autumn, the driving rain drummed on his sailcloth suit saturated almost to the stiffness of sheet-iron, with its surface flowing with water. When the weather was too bad, he retreated under the tiny porch, and, standing close against the door, looked at his spade left planted in the middle of the yard. The ground was so much dug up all over, that as the season advanced it turned to a quagmire. When it froze hard, he was disconsolate. What would Harry say? And as he could not have so much of Bessie's company at that time of the year, the roars of old Carvil, that came muffled through the closed windows, calling her indoors, exasperated him greatly.

" Why don't that extravagant fellow get you a servant? " he asked impatiently one mild afternoon. She had thrown something over her head to run out for a while.

" I don't know," said the pale Bessie, wearily, staring away with her heavy-lidded, grey, and unexpectant glance. There were always smudgy

[239]

shadows under her eyes, and she did not seem able
to see any change or any end to her life.

"You wait till you get married, my dear," said
her only friend, drawing closer to the fence.
"Harry will get you one."

His hopeful craze seemed to mock her own want
of hope with so bitter an aptness that in her nervous irritation she could have screamed at him out-
right. But she only said in self-mockery, and
speaking to him as though he had been sane,
"Why, Captain Hagberd, your son may not even
want to look at me."

He flung his head back and laughed his throaty
affected cackle of anger.

"What! That boy? Not want to look at the
only sensible girl for miles around? What do you
think I am here for, my dear—my dear—my dear?
. . . What? You wait. You just wait. You'll
see to-morrow. I'll soon——"

"Bessie! Bessie! Bessie!" howled old Carvil inside. "Bessie!—my pipe!" That fat blind man
had given himself up to a very lust of laziness. He
would not lift his hand to reach for the things she
took care to leave at his very elbow. He would not

[240]

move a limb; he would not rise from his chair, he would not put one foot before another, in that parlour (where he knew his way as well as if he had his sight), without calling her to his side and hanging all his atrocious weight on her shoulder. He would not eat one single mouthful of food without her close attendance. He had made himself helpless beyond his affliction, to enslave her better. She stood still for a moment, setting her teeth in the dusk, then turned and walked slowly indoors.

Captain Hagberd went back to his spade. The shouting in Carvil's cottage stopped, and after a while the window of the parlour downstairs was lit up. A man coming from the end of the street with a firm leisurely step passed on, but seemed to have caught sight of Captain Hagberd, because he turned back a pace or two. A cold white light lingered in the western sky. The man leaned over the gate in an interested manner.

"You must be Captain Hagberd," he said, with easy assurance.

The old man spun round, pulling out his spade, startled by the strange voice.

"Yes, I am," he answered nervously.

[241]

The other, smiling straight at him, uttered very slowly: " You've been advertising for your son, I believe? "

" My son Harry," mumbled Captain Hagberd, off his guard for once. " He's coming home to-morrow."

" The devil he is! " The stranger marvelled greatly, and then went on, with only a slight change of tone: " You've grown a beard like Father Christmas himself."

Captain Hagberd drew a little nearer, and leaned forward over his spade. " Go your way," he said, resentfully and timidly at the same time, because he was always afraid of being laughed at. Every mental state, even madness, has its equilibrium based upon self-esteem. Its disturbance causes unhappiness; and Captain Hagberd lived amongst a scheme of settled notions which it pained him to feel disturbed by people's grins. Yes, people's grins were awful. They hinted at something wrong: but what? He could not tell; and that stranger was obviously grinning—had come on purpose to grin. It was bad enough on the streets, but he had never before been outraged like this.

[242]

The stranger, unaware how near he was of having his head laid open with a spade, said seriously: "I am not trespassing where I stand, am I? I fancy there's something wrong about your news. Suppose you let me come in."

" *You* come in!" murmured old Hagberd, with inexpressible horror.

" I could give you some real information about your son—the very latest tip, if you care to hear."

" No," shouted Hagberd. He began to pace wildly to and fro, he shouldered his spade, he gesticulated with his other arm. " Here's a fellow— a grinning fellow, who says there's something wrong. I've got more information than you're aware of. I've all the information I want. I've had it for years—for years—for years—enough to last me till to-morrow. Let you come in, indeed! What would Harry say?"

Bessie Carvil's figure appeared in black silhouette on the parlour window; then, with the sound of an opening door, flitted out before the other cottage, all black, but with something white over her head. These two voices beginning to talk suddenly outside (she had heard them indoors) had given her such an emotion that she could not utter a sound.

Captain Hagberd seemed to be trying to find his way out of a cage. His feet squelched in the puddles left by his industry. He stumbled in the holes of the ruined grass-plot. He ran blindly against the fence.

" Here, steady a bit! " said the man at the gate, gravely stretching his arm over and catching him by the sleeve. " Somebody's been trying to get at you. Hallo! what's this rig you've got on? Storm canvas, by George! " He had a big laugh. " Well, you *are* a character! "

Captain Hagberd jerked himself free, and began to back away shrinkingly. " For the present," he muttered, in a crestfallen tone.

" What's the matter with him? " The stranger addressed Bessie with the utmost familiarity, in a deliberate, explanatory tone. " I didn't want to startle the old man." He lowered his voice as though he had known her for years. " I dropped into a barber's on my way, to get a twopenny shave, and they told me there he was something of a character. The old man has been a character all his life."

Captain Hagberd, daunted by the allusion to his clothing, had retreated inside, taking his spade with him; and the two at the gate, startled by the unexpected slamming of the door, heard the bolts being shot, the snapping of the lock, and the echo of an affected gurgling laugh within.

"I didn't want to upset him," the man said, after a short silence. "What's the meaning of all this? He isn't quite crazy."

"He has been worrying a long time about his lost son," said Bessie, in a low, apologetic tone.

"Well, I am his son."

"Harry!" she cried—and was profoundly silent.

"Know my name? Friends with the old man, eh?"

"He's our landlord," Bessie faltered out, catching hold of the iron railing.

"Owns both them rabbit-hutches, does he?" commented young Hagberd, scornfully; "just the thing he would be proud of. Can you tell me who's that chap coming to-morrow? You must know

[245]

something of it. I tell you, it's a swindle on the old man—nothing else."

She did not answer, helpless before an insurmountable difficulty, appalled before the necessity, the impossibility and the dread of an explanation in which she and madness seemed involved together.

" Oh—I am so sorry," she murmured.

" What's the matter? " he said, with serenity. " You needn't be afraid of upsetting me. It's the other fellow that'll be upset when he least expects it. I don't care a hang; but there will be some fun when he shows his mug to-morrow. I don't care *that* for the old man's pieces, but right is right. You shall see me put a head on that coon—whoever he is! "

He had come nearer, and towered above her on the other side of the railings. He glanced at her hands. He fancied she was trembling, and it occurred to him that she had her part perhaps in that little game that was to be sprung on his old man to-morrow. He had come just in time to spoil their sport. He was entertained by the idea—scornful of the baffled plot. But all his life he had been full of indulgence for all sorts of women's tricks. She

[246]

really was trembling very much; her wrap had slipped off her head. " Poor devil!" he thought. " Never mind about that chap. I daresay he'll change his mind before to-morrow. But what about me? I can't loaf about the gate til the morning."

She burst out: " It is *you*—you yourself that he's waiting for. It is *you* who come to-morrow."

He murmured. " Oh! It's me!" blankly, and they seemed to become breathless together. Apparently he was pondering over what he had heard; then, without irritation, but evidently perplexed, he said: " I don't understand. I hadn't written or anything. It's my chum who saw the paper and told me—this very morning. . . . Eh? what?"

He bent his ear; she whispered rapidly, and he listened for a while, muttering the words " yes " and " I see " at times. Then, " But why won't to-day do?" he queried at last.

"You didn't understand me!" she exclaimed, impatiently. The clear streak of light under the clouds died out in the west. Again he stooped slightly to hear better; and the deep night buried everything of the whispering woman and the attentive man, except the familiar contiguity of their faces, with its air of secrecy and caress.

He squared his shoulders; the broad-brimmed shadow of a hat sat cavalierly on his head. " Awkward this, eh? " he appealed to her. " To-morrow? Well, well! Never heard tell of anything like this. It's all to-morrow, then, without any sort of to-day, as far as I can see."

She remained still and mute.

" And you have been encouraging this funny notion," he said.

" I never contradicted him."

" Why didn't you? "

" What for should I? " she defended herself. " It would only have made him miserable. He would have gone out of his mind."

" His mind! " he muttered, and heard a short nervous laugh from her.

" Where was the harm? Was I to quarrel with the poor old man? It was easier to half believe it myself."

" Aye, aye," he meditated, intelligently. " I suppose the old chap got around you somehow with his soft talk. You are good-hearted."

Her hands moved up in the dark nervously. "And it might have been true. It was true. It has come. Here it is. This is the to-morrow we have been waiting for."

She drew a breath, and he said, good-humouredly: "Aye, with the door shut. I wouldn't care if . . . And you think he could be brought round to recognise me . . . Eh? What? . . . You could do it? In a week you say? H'm, I daresay you could—but do you think I could hold out a week in this dead-alive place? Not me! I want either hard work, or an all-fired racket, or more space than there is in the whole of England. I have been in this place, though, once before, and for more than a week. The old man was advertising for me then, and a chum I had with me had a notion of getting a couple of quid out of him by writing a lot of silly nonsense in a letter. That lark did not come off, though. We had to clear out—and none too soon. But this time I've a chum waiting for me in London, and besides . . ."

Bessie Carvil was breathing quickly.

"What if I tried a knock at the door?" he suggested.

"Try," she said.

Captain Hagberd's gate squeaked, and the shadow of the son moved on, then stopped with another deep laugh in the throat, like the father's, only soft and gentle, thrilling to the woman's heart, awakening to her ears.

"He isn't frisky—is he? I would be afraid to lay hold of him. The chaps are always telling me I don't know my own strength."

"He's the most harmless creature that ever lived," she interrupted.

"You wouldn't say so if you had seen him chasing me upstairs with a hard leather strap," he said; "I haven't forgotten it in sixteen years."

She got warm from head to foot under another soft, subdued laugh. At the rat-tat-tat of the knocker her heart flew into her mouth.

"Hey, dad! Let me in. I am Harry, I am. Straight! Come back home a day too soon."

One of the windows upstairs ran up.

"A grinning, information fellow," said the voice of old Hagberd, up in the darkness. "Don't you have anything to do with him. It will spoil everything."

[250]

She heard Harry Hagberd say, " Hallo, dad," then a clanging clatter. The window rumbled down, and he stood before her again.

" It's just like old times. Nearly walloped the life out of me to stop me going away, and now I come back he throws a confounded shovel at my head to keep me out. It grazed my shoulder."

She shuddered.

" I wouldn't care," he began, " only I spent my last shillings on the railway fare and my last two-pence on a shave—out of respect for the old man."

" Are you really Harry Hagberd? " she asked, he said, jovially. " Prove with what? What do I

" Can I prove it? Can any one else prove it? " he said jovially. " Prove with what? What do I want to prove? There isn't a single corner in the world, barring England, perhaps, where you could not find some man, or more likely woman, that would remember me for Harry Hagberd. I am more like Harry Hagberd than any man alive; and I can prove it to you in a minute, if you will let me step inside your gate."

" Come in," she said.

He entered then the front garden of the Carvils.

[251]

His tall shadow strode with a swagger; she turned her back on the window and waited, watching the shape, of which the footfalls seemed the most material part. The light fell on a tilted hat; a powerful shoulder, that seemed to cleave the darkness; on a leg stepping out. He swung about and stood still, facing the illuminated parlour window at her back, turning his head from side to side, laughing softly to himself.

" Just fancy, for a minute, the old man's beard stuck on to my chin. Hey? Now say. I was the very spit of him from a boy."

" It's true," she murmured to herself.

" And that's about as far as it goes. He was always one of your domestic characters. Why, I remember how he used to go about looking very sick for three days before he had to leave home on one of his trips to South Shields for coal. He had a standing charter from the gas-works. You would think he was off on a whaling cruise—three years and a tail. Ha, ha! Not a bit of it. Ten days on the outside. The *Skimmer of the Seas* was a smart craft. Fine name, wasn't it? Mother's uncle owned her. . . ."

He interrupted himself, and in a lowered voice, "Did he ever tell you what mother died of?" he asked.

"Yes," said Miss Bessie, bitterly; "from impatience."

He made no sound for a while; then brusquely: "They were so afraid I would turn out badly that they fairly drove me away. Mother nagged at me for being idle, and the old man said he would cut my soul out of my body rather than let me go to sea. Well, it looked as if he would do it too—so I went. It looks to me sometimes as if I had been born to them by a mistake—in that other hutch of a house."

"Where ought you to have been born by rights?" Bessie Carvil interrupted him, defiantly.

"In the open, upon a beach, on a windy night," he said, quick as lightning. Then he mused slowly. "They were characters, both of them, by George; and the old man keeps it up well—don't he? A damned shovel on the——Hark! who's that making that row? 'Bessie, Bessie.' It's in your house."

"It's for me," she said, with indifference.

He stepped aside, out of the streak of light. "Your husband?" he inquired, with the tone of a man accustomed to unlawful trysts. "Fine voice for a ship's deck in a thundering squall."

"No; my father. I am not married."

"You seem a fine girl, Miss Bessie, dear," he said at once.

She turned her face away.

"Oh, I say,—what's up? Who's murdering him?"

"He wants his tea." She faced him, still and tall, with averted head, with her hands hanging clasped before her.

"Hadn't you better go in?" he suggested, after watching for a while the nape of her neck, a patch of dazzling white skin and soft shadow above the sombre line of her shoulders. Her wrap had slipped down to her elbows. "You'll have all the town coming out presently. I'll wait here a bit."

Her wrap fell to the ground, and he stooped to pick it up; she had vanished. He threw it over his arm, and approaching the window squarely he saw a monstrous form of a fat man in an arm-chair, an unshaded lamp, the yawning of an enor-

mous mouth in a big flat face encircled by a ragged
halo of hair—Miss Bessie's head and bust. The
shouting stopped; the blind ran down. He lost
himself in thinking how awkward it was. Father
mad; no getting into the house. No money to get
back; a hungry chum in London who would begin
to think he had been given the go-by. "Damn!"
he muttered. He could break the door in, certainly; but they would perhaps bundle him into
chokey for that without asking questions—no great
matter, only he was confoundedly afraid of being
locked up, even in mistake. He turned cold at the
thought. He stamped his feet on the sod-
den grass.

"What are you?—a sailor?" said an agitated
voice.

She had flitted out, a shadow herself, attracted
by the reckless shadow waiting under the wall of
her home.

"Anything. Enough of a sailor to be worth
my salt before the mast. Came home that way this
time."

"Where do you come from?" she asked.

"Right away from a jolly good spree," he said,

" by the London train—see? Ough! I hate being shut up in a train. I don't mind a house so much."

" Ah," she said; " that's lucky."

" Because in a house you can at any time open the blamed door and walk away straight before you."

" And never come back? "

" Not for sixteen years at least," he laughed. " To a rabbit hutch, and get a confounded old shovel . . ."

" A ship is not so very big," she taunted.

" No, but the sea is great."

She dropped her head, and as if her ears had been opened to the voices of the world, she heard, beyond the rampart of sea-wall, the swell of yesterday's gale breaking on the beach with monotonous and solemn vibrations, as if all the earth had been a tolling bell.

" And then, why, a ship's a ship. You love her and leave her; and a voyage isn't a marriage." He quoted the sailor's saying lightly.

" It is not a marriage," she whispered.

" I never took a false name, and I've never yet

told a lie to a woman. What lie? Why, *the* lie———.
Take me or leave me, I say: and if you take me,
then it is . . ." He hummed a snatch very low,
leaning against the wall.

> *Oh, ho, ho Rio!*
> *And fare thee well,*
> *My bonnie young girl,*
> *We're bound to Rio Grande.*

" Capstan song," he explained. Her teeth chattered.

" You are cold," he said. " Here's that affair
of yours I picked up." She felt his hands about
her, wrapping her closely. " Hold the ends together in front," he commanded.

" What did you come here for? " she asked, re-
pressing a shudder.

" Five quid," he answered, promptly. " We let
our spree go on a little too long and got hard up."

" You've been drinking? " she said.

" Blind three days; on purpose. I am not given
that way—don't you think. There's nothing and
nobody that can get over me unless I like. I can

be as steady as a rock. My chum sees the paper this morning, and says he to me: ' Go on, Harry: loving parent. That's five quid sure.' So we scraped all our pockets for the fare. Devil of a lark!"

" You have a hard heart, I am afraid," she sighed.

" What for? For running away? Why! he wanted to make a lawyer's clerk of me—just to please himself. Master in his own house; and my poor mother egged him on—for my good, I suppose. Well, then—so long; and I went. No, I tell you: the day I cleared out, I was all black and blue from his great fondness for me. Ah! he was always a bit of a character. Look at that shovel now. Off his chump? Not much. That's just exactly like my dad. He wants me here just to have somebody to order about. However, we two were hard up; and what's five quid to him—once in sixteen hard years? "

" Oh, but I am sorry for you. Did you never want to come back home? "

" Be a lawyer's clerk and rot here—in some such place as this? " he cried in contempt. " What! if

the old man set me up in a home to-day, I would
kick it down about my ears—or else die there before the third day was out."

" And where else is it that you hope to die? "

" In the bush somewhere; in the sea; on a blamed
mountain-top for choice. At home? Yes! the
world's my home; but I expect I'll die in a hospital
some day. What of that? Any place is good
enough, as long as I've lived; and I've been everything you can think of almost but a tailor or a
soldier. I've been a boundary rider; I've sheared
sheep; and humped my swag; and harpooned a
whale. I've rigged ships, and prospected for gold,
and skinned dead bullocks,—and turned my back
on more money than the old man would have
scraped in his whole life. Ha, ha!"

He overwhelmed her. She pulled herself together and managed to utter, " Time to rest
now."

He straightened himself up, away from the wall,
and in a severe voice said, " Time to go."

But he did not move. He leaned back again,
and hummed thoughtfully a bar or two of an outlandish tune.

She felt as if she were about to cry. "That's another of your cruel songs," she said.

"Learned it in Mexico—in Sonora." He talked easily. "It is the song of the Gambucinos. You don't know? The song of restless men. Nothing could hold them in one place—not even a woman. You used to meet one of them now and again, in the old days, on the edge of the gold country, away north there beyond the Rio Gila. I've seen it. A prospecting engineer in Mazatlan took me along with him to help look after the waggons. A sailor's a handy chap to have about you anyhow. It's all a desert: cracks in the earth that you can't see the bottom of; and mountains—sheer rocks standing up high like walls and church spires, only a hundred times bigger. The valleys are full of boulders and black stones. There's not a blade of grass to see; and the sun sets more red over that country than I have seen it anywhere—blood-red and angry. It *is* fine."

"You do not want to go back there again?" she stammered out.

He laughed a little. "No. That's the blamed gold country. It gave me the shivers sometimes to look at it—and we were a big lot of men together, mind; but these Gambucinos wandered alone. They knew that country before anybody had ever heard of it. They had a sort of gift for prospecting, and the fever of it was on them too; and they did not seem to want the gold very much. They would find some rich spot, and then turn their backs on it; pick up perhaps a little—enough for a spree—and then be off again, looking for more. They never stopped long where there were houses; they had no wife, no chick, no home, never a chum. You couldn't be friends with a Gambucino; they were too restless—here to-day, and gone, God knows where, to-morrow. They told no one of their finds, and there has never been a Gambucino well off. It was not for the gold they cared; it was the wandering about looking for it in the stony country that got into them and wouldn't let them rest; so that no woman yet born could hold a Gambucino for more than a week. That's what the song says. It's all about a pretty girl that tried hard to keep hold of a Gambucino lover, so that he should bring her lots of gold. No fear! Off he went, and she never saw him again."

"What became of her?" she breathed out.

"The song don't tell. Cried a bit, I daresay. They were the fellows: kiss and go. But it's the looking for a thing—a something . . . Sometimes I think I am a sort of Gambucino myself."

"No woman can hold you, then," she began in a brazen voice, which quavered suddenly before the end.

"No longer than a week," he joked, playing upon her very heartstrings with the gay, tender note of his laugh; "and yet I am fond of them all. Anything for a woman of the right sort. The scrapes they got me into, and the scrapes they got me out of! I love them at first sight. I've fallen in love with you already, Miss—Bessie's your name—eh?"

She backed away a little, and with a trembling laugh:

"You haven't seen my face yet."

He bent forward gallantly. "A little pale: it suits some. But you are a fine figure of a girl, Miss Bessie."

She was all in a flutter. Nobody had ever said so much to her before.

His tone changed. "I am getting middling hungry, though. Had no breakfast to-day. Couldn't you scare up some bread from that tea for me, or——"

She was gone already. He had been on the point of asking her to let him come inside. No matter. Anywhere would do. Devil of a fix! What would his chum think?

"I didn't ask you as a beggar," he said, jestingly, taking a piece of bread-and-butter from the plate she held before him. "I asked as a friend. My dad is rich, you know."

"He starves himself for your sake."

"And I have starved for his whim," he said, taking up another piece.

"All he has in the world is for you," she pleaded.

"Yes, if I come here to sit on it like a dam' toad in a hole. Thank you; and what about the shovel, eh? He always had a queer way of showing his love."

"I could bring him round in a week," she suggested, timidly.

He was too hungry to answer her; and, holding

[263]

the plate submissively to his hand, she began to whisper up to him in a quick, panting voice. He listened, amazed, eating slower and slower, till at last his jaws stopped altogether. "That's his game, is it?" he said, in a rising tone of scathing contempt. An ungovernable movement of his arm sent the plate flying out of her fingers. He shot out a violent curse.

She shrank from him, putting her hand against the wall.

"No!" he raged. "He expects! Expects *me* —for his rotten money! . . . . Who wants his home? Mad—not he! Don't you think. He wants his own way. He wanted to turn me into a miserable lawyer's clerk, and now he wants to make of me a blamed tame rabbit in a cage. Of me! Of me!" His subdued angry laugh frightened her now.

"The whole world ain't a bit too big for me to spread my elbows in, I can tell you—what's your name—Bessie—let alone a dam' parlour in a hutch. Marry! He wants me to marry and settle! And as likely as not he has looked out the girl too—

dash my soul! And do you know the Judy, may I ask?"

She shook all over with noiseless dry sobs; but he was fuming and fretting too much to notice her distress. He bit his thumb with rage at the mere idea. A window rattled up.

"A grinning, information fellow," pronounced old Hagberd dogmatically, in measured tones. And the sound of his voice seemed to Bessie to make the night itself mad—to pour insanity and disaster on the earth. "Now I know what's wrong with the people here, my dear. Why, of course! With this mad chap going about. Don't you have anything to do with him, Bessie. Bessie, I say!"

They stood as if dumb. The old man fidgeted and mumbled to himself at the window. Suddenly he cried, piercingly: "Bessie—I see you. I'll tell Harry."

She made a movement as if to run away, but stopped and raised her hands to her temples. Young Hagberd, shadowy and big, stirred no more than a man of bronze. Over their heads the crazy night whimpered and scolded in an old man's voice.

[265]

" Send him away, my dear. He's only a vaga-
bond. What you want is a good home of your own.
That chap has no home—he's not like Harry. He
can't be Harry. Harry is coming to-morrow. Do
you hear? One day more," he babbled more ex-
citedly; "never you fear—Harry shall marry
you."

His voice rose very shrill and mad against the
regular deep soughing of the swell coiling heavily
about the outer face of the sea-wall.

" He will have to. I shall make him, or if not "
—he swore a great oath—" I'll cut him off with a
shilling to-morrow, and leave everything to you.
I shall. To you. Let him starve."

The window rattled down.

Harry drew a deep breath, and took one step
toward Bessie. " So it's you—the girl," he said,
in a lowered voice. She had not moved, and she remained half turned away from him, pressing the
palms of her hands. " My word!" he continued,
with an invisible half-smile on his lips. " I have a
great mind to stop. . . ."

Her elbows were trembling violently.

" For a week," he finished without a pause.

She clapped her hands to her face.

He came up quite close, and took hold of her wrists gently. She felt his breath on her ear.

" It's a scrape I am in—this, and it is you that must see me through." He was trying to uncover her face. She resisted. He let her go then, and stepping back a little, " Have you got any money? " he asked. " I must be off now."

She nodded quickly her shamefaced head, and he waited, looking away from her, while, trembling all over and bowing her neck, she tried to find the pocket of her dress.

" Here it is! " she whispered. " Oh, go away! go away for God's sake! If I had more—more— I would give it all to forget—to make you forget."

He extended his hand. " No fear! I haven't forgotten a single one of you in the world. Some gave me more than money—but I am a beggar now —and you women always had to get me out of my scrapes."

He swaggered up to the parlour window, and in the dim light filtering through the blind, looked at the coin lying in his palm. It was a half-sovereign.

He slipped it into his pocket. She stood a little on one side, with her head drooping, as if wounded; with her arms hanging passive by her side, as if dead.

"You can't buy me in," he said, "and you can't buy yourself out."

He set his hat firmly with a little tap, and next moment she felt herself lifted up in the powerful embrace of his arms. Her feet lost the ground; her head hung back; he showered kisses on her face with a silent and over-mastering ardour, as if in haste to get at her very soul. He kissed her pale cheeks, her hard forehead, her heavy eyelids, her faded lips; and the measured blows and sighs of the rising tide accompanied the enfolding power of his arms, the overwhelming might of his caresses. It was as if the sea, breaking down the wall protecting all the homes of the town, had sent a wave over her head. It passed on; she staggered backwards, with her shoulders against the wall, exhausted, as if she had been stranded there after a storm and a shipwreck.

She opened her eyes after awhile; and listening to the firm, leisurely footsteps going away with their conquest, began to gather her skirts, staring all the time before her. Suddenly she darted through the open gate into the dark and deserted street.

" Stop! " she shouted. " Don't go! "

And listening with an attentive poise of the head, she could not tell whether it was the beat of the swell or his fateful tread that seemed to fall cruelly upon her heart. Presently every sound grew fainter, as though she were slowly turning into stone. A fear of this awful silence came to her— worse than the fear of death. She called upon her ebbing strength for the final appeal:

" Harry! "

Not even the dying echo of a footstep. Nothing. The thundering of the surf, the voice of the restless sea itself, seemed stopped. There was not a sound—no whisper of life, as though she were alone and lost in that stony country of which she had heard, where madmen go looking for gold and spurn the find.

Captain Hagberd, inside his dark house, had kept on the alert. A window ran up; and in the silence of the stony country a voice spoke above her head, high up in the black air—the voice of madness, lies and despair—the voice of inextinguishable hope. "Is he gone yet—that information fellow? Do you hear him about, my dear?"

She burst into tears. "No! no! no! I don't hear him any more," she sobbed.

He began to chuckle up there triumphantly. "You frightened him away. Good girl. Now we shall be all right. Don't you be impatient, my dear. One day more."

In the other house old Carvil, wallowing regally in his arm-chair, with a globe lamp burning by his side on the table, yelled for her, in a fiendish voice: "Bessie! Bessie! you Bessie!"

She heard him at last, and, as if overcome by fate, began to totter silently back toward her stuffy little inferno of a cottage. It had no lofty portal, no terrific inscription of forfeited hopes—she did not understand wherein she had sinned.

Captain Hagberd had gradually worked himself into a state of noisy happiness up there.

"Go in! Keep quiet!" she turned upon him tearfully, from the doorstep below.

He rebelled against her authority in his great

joy at having got rid at last of that " something wrong." It was as if all the hopeful madness of the world had broken out to bring terror upon her heart, with the voice of that old man shouting of his trust in an everlasting to-morrow.

THE END

By Stanley J. Weyman

Author of "A Gentleman of France"
THE LONG NIGHT

GENEVA in the early days of the 17th century; a ruffling young theologue new to the city; a beautiful and innocent girl, suspected of witchcraft; a crafty scholar and metaphysician seeking to give over the city into the hands of the Savoyards; a stern and powerful syndic whom the scholar beguiles to betray his office by promises of an elixir which shall save him from his fatal illness; a brutal soldier of fortune; these are the elements of which Weyman has composed the most brilliant and thrilling of his romances. Claude Mercier, the student, seeing the plot in which the girl he loves is involved, yet helpless to divulge it, finds at last his opportunity when the treacherous men of Savoy are admitted within Geneva's walls, and in a night of whirlwind fighting saves the city by his courage and address. For fire and spirit there are few chapters in modern literature such as those which picture the splendid defence of Geneva, by the staid, churchly, heroic burghers, fighting in their own blood under the divided leadership of the fat Syndic, Baudichon, and the bandy-legged sailor, Jehan Brosse, winning the battle against the armed and armored forces of the invaders.

Illustrated by Solomon J. Solomon.
$1.50

McClure, Phillips & Co.